A Roast

on

Sunday

By Tammy
Robinson

This book is set in New Zealand and as such all spelling is in New Zealand English.

Acknowledgments

A HUGE thank you to my early readers, Kerrie Ryan, Cara Randall-Hunt, Richard James Lloyd, Miriam Byrne and Andrea Sheffield, for your feedback and editing skills. The love you guys had for the characters gave me the encouragement to keep writing the story.

Also a GINORMOUS thank you to my clever husband Karl for his fantastic editing skills and cover design. Also for coming home from a full day at work and feeding and bathing the baby so I could get some more writing done.

This book is dedicated to our beautiful, incredible, gorgeous, clever, adorable and amazing daughter Holly. If your attitude and feistiness now at one year old is any indication, we're in for some fun (i.e. trouble) with you!

Love you so much baby girl

Chapter one

To an ignorant observer it would appear that the girl was merely sat on the shore enjoying the view. Only once you got close enough could you hear her muttering, although the words themselves were undecipherable, snatched by the breeze as soon as they emerged from her lips and carried off into the trees that rimmed the lake.

She had the lake to herself, thanks to the early morning chill in the air. On hot days this place was packed with families enjoying picnics and the water, and teenagers secretly enjoying the sight of the opposite sex and their burgeoning bodies. But on cold mornings like this most stayed away, apart from dog walkers, bird watchers and other odd, outdoorsy types.

"I'd like to see how she'd manage without me," the girl said, scowling and kicking out at a nearby rock.

Earlier on the shore she had traced the length of the waterline, as the best pebbles and stones were usually to be found there. On other days, when she had time and no plan to be gotten on with she enjoyed taking it slowly, collecting only the best specimens which now lined the windowsill in her bedroom. They caught the afternoon sun and cast interesting patterns on her walls. Those days she liked to focus on picking the ones with the prettiest colours, or patterns. Not perfect rocks mind you; she liked them to have some kind of minor imperfection, a chip or a crack perhaps.

But today she had a job to do and limited time to do it in. So she settled for any old rocks, green ones with flecks of black, grey with holes like the craters of the moon. Weight was what she was after so she threw any that she considered too light into the water. She didn't even have time today to try and better her skimming score, (for the record she had once achieved nine perfect surface skims, although her best friend Nick refused to allow it into their record book as it had not been witnessed by him. Jerk.)

When she had filled her mother's linen shopping bag with enough stones she settled on the shore and sorted through them, once again weighing them between her hands, tossing any that were too small or light, and filling the pockets on her raincoat with the rest.

The raincoat was a sore point, and the girl normally never voluntarily wore it. In fact, she hated it with a seething passion and had tried to lose it on numerous occasions, but the damn thing had a habit of turning back up. Of course it didn't help that her mother had written her name in big black letters on the outside of the collar, right there where everyone could see it. Tags you could cut out, but permanent marker wasn't so easy to remove. She'd tried scrubbing it off with soap, and bleaching it off with the stuff her mother used to clean the toilet, but it was like it was retardant to all her efforts.

"You have got to be kidding me," she'd said last winter when her grandmother had passed it to her with a flourish one morning over breakfast, with an expression the girl could only describe as mildly evil; mirth dancing a foxtrot around her lips. Her grandmother was good at that, chucking fuel on a fire and watching situations explode. She wasn't a bad person as such, but she had a streak of mischievousness a mile wide in her. The coat was bright pink with giant cheerful strawberries, complete with faces, splashed across it. The girl hadn't worn anything pink since she'd been old enough to dress herself and she had no intention of starting again. What made it even worse was that the girl had red hair. Red like the colour of a cornfield at sunset. A pink coat on a kid with red hair? Her grandmother may as well have bought her a sandwich board to wear saying 'Please pick on me!' and been done with it.

"Like hell am I wearing that," the girl had said.

"Don't swear," her mother had admonished her.

"Ok, like *sugar* will I ever be caught dead wearing that, better?"

"Better. But yes, you are wearing it."

"I'm not."

"You are."

"You can't make me."

Her mother had sighed. "No, I can't make you. But I can't afford to buy you a new jacket either, so you either wear it or you freeze. Up to you. And before you tell me you don't give a sugar if you freeze, think of your grandmother. You don't want to hurt her feelings do you?"

The girl looked at her grandmother, who did her best to look hurt. The girl sighed.

"Fine. Whatever," she'd said, although she intended on losing it at the first opportunity possible. She'd left the coat on buses, up trees, stuffed into a post box and once she'd even hurled it into a creek and watched it get carried away with the current, but somehow it always came back. If she didn't know better she'd think the stupid thing was possessed.

She'd worn the coat to the lake today because it was the only thing she owned with deep enough pockets. She managed to fit thirty stones into her left pocket and twenty eight into the right, and when she stumbled to her feet she nearly pitched over backwards.

"Perfect," she declared.

With one last glance along the shore to make sure she was alone, she walked, or rather lurched, into the water and headed straight out until just her head was left poking out above the surface.

"Here goes," she said, taking a deep breath, and she took another step forward until the water closed over her head

4

and only ripples were left, fanning out in circles that got bigger and fainter and eventually disappeared.

Chapter Two

She had failed to notice the man and his dog emerging from the tree line on the hill directly behind her. He liked walking at this early time of the morning. A chance to clear his head and prepare himself for whatever madness the day ahead might bring.

The dog was as black as a starless night sky, and tall, reaching almost to the man's waist. Despite his intimidating size, his expression was one of docile friendliness, a long pink tongue lolling out one side of his mouth between pointed and yellowing teeth.

The man watched the girl wade clumsily out into the water. Curious, he thought, perhaps that was what they did in these parts; swim in raincoats. It wouldn't surprise him. He'd only moved here a few months back and only from a few hundred kilometres away but some days he felt like he'd been transplanted into a strange new world. People round here were, *different.* There really was no other word for it. No polite one anyway.

He watched as the ripples dispersed and waited with interest for the girl to surface again. The dog pulled impatiently on the leash; he wanted to head home to where his bowl was waiting to be filled with breakfast.

When she hadn't popped up after twenty seconds he started to worry, and another twenty seconds later he started running for the shore, dropping the leash as he did. The dog sighed, sensing that breakfast had just taken a giant step backwards.

Without stopping to remove any clothing the man plunged into the water and headed for the spot where he'd last seen her. As his boots filed with water and started to drag him down he wished he'd taken the time to stop and remove them, but he knew there had been no time. He took a quick breath and dived under the surface, opening his eyes and peering through the gloom for some sign of the girl. The water was cold, colder than he was prepared for and he felt his skin spring up into a million goose bumps, and his ribs contract in protest. Visibility was poor and he could see only a metre or so in front of him. The water was a dark, murky green, with floating white specks and when he moved he stirred them up like a snowstorm and they swirled around him like angry bees.

He couldn't see her and his lungs were crying out for air, so he surfaced and gulped in the air thirstily. Shit, he thought, where the hell was she? He turned on the spot to see if she had surfaced without his knowledge but there was no sign of her. Just as he was about to dive back down he noticed them; a trail of bubbles popping to the surface, only a few metres to his right. He took a few strokes until he was in the same spot and then taking another deep breath he dove under. This time he could see her. She was on the bottom of the lake, a few metres down. If it hadn't been for her jacket he may not have spotted her, but the faces on the strawberries beamed up at him from the murky deep. Using his hands and body and he pushed himself down towards the bottom until he could reach her. When he put a hand on her shoulder she spun as quickly as the water would allow and seeing him she swore; he couldn't hear it under water but there was no mistaking the shape of her mouth. She pushed his hand off her shoulder and tried to move away from him but he reached out and grabbed her again, even though his lungs were screaming. He was not leaving her down here to drown, that he knew for certain. If he surfaced now he may not be able to find her again, and he couldn't live with that on his conscience. She tried to shrug his hand off again but he gripped her and gestured towards the surface.

Later on, when he was reliving the experience while trying to get some warmth back into his body in the shower, he could have sworn that in that moment she had rolled her eyes at him.

Underwater.

She started to shrug her arms out of the jacket and he helped her, yanking at one sleeve till her hand popped out the other end. Then she was gone, kicking up towards the surface, and he dropped the oddly heavy jacket and kicked off after her.

She broke through the surface first, and without waiting for him she struck out for the shore. Breaking through himself he took a large gulp of air and then he swam to catch up. He waited until they were back on the shore before he finally spoke.

"Just what the hell do you think you're playing at?" he asked her furiously.

"Me?" she blinked at him in surprise and retaliated anger. "You're the one with the problem mister. *You* came after *me,* remember."

"Of course I did, I was hardly going to leave you to drown down there."

She frowned at him. "I was hardly going to drown."

"I hate to break it to you but that's typically what happens when someone stays under the water as long as you did without breathing."

"Well duh, I'm not an idiot."

"What were you doing down there?"

She held out a hand and in it he could see a small piece of lake weed; vivid green and stark against the paleness of her palm.

"Not that it's any of your business," she said, "but I was picking this. Now you and your stupid David Hasselhoff rescue efforts have made me drop the rest of it. Nice one."

"You were picking weed?"

"Gee, quick on the uptake aren't you," she said.

"Smart arse, aren't you?"

She poked her tongue out at him.

"What do you want the weed for anyway?" he asked, trying to wring some of the water from his trousers.

"Like I said, it's none of your business."

Something else occurred to him. "How did you manage to stay underwater for so long without breathing? You were down there for a very long time."

She shrugged but didn't answer.

'I know," he said, "it's none of my business right."

The girl nodded approvingly. "Now you're catching on quicker." Her attention became distracted by the dog that had joined his master's side. The dog stared up at the man mournfully, trying to convey the hunger that was greatly troubling him.

"Nice dog," she said. "Yours?"

"Thanks, and yes, he's mine."

"What's his name?"

"Rufus."

"What a terrible name for a dog."

"Agreed. I didn't name him."

"Who did?"

"Now who's being nosy?"

"Fine, don't tell me. I don't care."

He chuckled, she was a touch prickly this kid. "My ex-girlfriend named him."

The girl regarded the dog thoughtfully.

"He looks like an Apollo," she said.

And the man thought; she's right. He *does* look like an Apollo.

"He looks like a pretty clever dog," the girl continued.

"He is."

The girl crossed her arms. "Looks like the kind of dog who knows when to mind his own business."

Forget his earlier estimation he thought, she was a hell of a lot prickly.

"Point taken," he said.

"Good, now get lost."

He raised an eyebrow at her but she refused to be intimidated. "I don't think so," he said. "I'd like to have a word to your parents about what just happened."

The girl shrugged again, "be my guest," she said. But she had no intention of letting him see where she lived, so she led him on a merry dance around town, starting with the school, winding in and out of the classrooms, turning occasionally to smile crookedly at him over her shoulder. He was still close behind her though when she reached the edge of the field so she took him over to Main Street, crossing from the left side of the road to the right side and then back again, every twenty metres or so. Still, he didn't give up, so she finally decided screw it, he could be her mother's problem. She was cold and hungry and fed up, so she left town, walking up the dirt road that led to her house. She stomped up the porch and entered the house, letting the screen door slam shut behind her.

Her mother's head popped out of the kitchen.

"That took awhile, you ok?"

"I'm fine."

Her mother noticed her empty hands.

"Did you leave it outside?"

The girl fumbled to get her hand into her jean pocket, made more difficult by the fact they were still wet and were drying onto her body like stiff cardboard.

"Here," she said, throwing the small piece of weed at her mother.

"Where's the rest of it?"

The girl thumbed over her shoulder. "Ask that idiot," then she stomped off up the stairs to run herself a hot bath. She had a date with a book; her mother could deal with the man outside.

There was the sound of a throat clearing at the screen door.

"I think she's referring to me," the man said.

Her mother crossed the room but didn't open the door. She checked the man carefully for signs of danger. He didn't look dangerous, but then again, what exactly did danger look like?

"I have a gun," she finally said, opening the screen door enough so they could appraise each other properly, but not enough to invite him over the threshold.

"Right. That's good to know."

"Who are you and what do you want?"

"Can I come in? It's a bit breezy out here and I'm wet through from trying to save your daughter."

"Save her from what?"

"Drowning."

The girl's mother turned towards the stairs and yelled out, "Willow, get back down here."

A minute later the girls face appeared in the doorway.

"What?" she asked.

"I asked if you were ok and you didn't tell me you nearly drowned. That's the kind of thing I'd like to know."

"That's because I didn't 'nearly drown'. I was fine, just doing what I always do. He," she jerked her head towards the man on the other side of the door, "decided to play lifeguard and swam in to haul me out."

Her mother turned back to the man. "Look, Mr -?"

"Cartwright, but call me Jack."

"- Mr Cartwright, I appreciate your concern and your lifesaving efforts, but I'm sure my daughter was perfectly fine. She's an excellent swimmer."

"That may be, but she wasn't exactly swimming. She was picking lake weed. From the *bottom of a lake.*"

"Yes, I know. And?"

"Sorry, but am I the only one who thinks there's something slightly odd about that?"

"Look, I appreciate your concern, but my daughter can look after herself in the water. Thank you for seeing her home safely, but you can leave now."

"Mrs -?"

"Tanner."

"Do you have a first name?"

"Maggie," she said reluctantly, "but you can call me Mrs Tanner."

He was starting to see where Willow got her attitude from.

"Mrs Tanner, I don't think its normal behaviour for a kid wearing a raincoat to walk out into a lake to pick weed. I know this town is strange, but even that's going a bit far."

Both mother and daughter bristled at the word 'strange'. This town was their home, and its melting pot of people their extended family. A stranger calling them strange was like a slap to the face.

14

"I think you should leave now," Maggie said, arms crossed defensively in front of her.

"Yeah, get lost," Willow added.

"Has anyone ever told you that your kid has a bad attitude?" the man said, leaning against the doorframe.

Willow sucked in her breath. Now he'd done it. Her mother could put up with a lot but she wouldn't *stand* for anyone saying a bad word about her only daughter. Her mother was super protective.

"Willow, go and have your bath," her mother said without turning.

"Aw but-" Willow wanted to stay and watch the fireworks.

"Go."

Reluctantly, Willow left. But before she disappeared completely from sight she turned and poked her tongue out at the man.

"Nice," he said, "really mature."

"How dare you," Maggie hissed when they were alone again.

"How dare I what, exactly?" He was enjoying the verbal sparring. The first thing he'd noticed when she'd come to the door was that Maggie was a remarkably attractive woman. Long mahogany coloured hair reached almost to her waist which was small and nipped in nicely before curving out over her hips. Her features were delicate and refined, and she had a dimple in her chin which he found fascinating. Since she'd gotten angry with him she had become even more alive. He wanted to continue fanning the embers and see just how animated she would get.

"How dare you judge us when you don't know the first thing about us," she said. "It's people like *you* who come into this town and bring gossip and trouble with you."

"First of all, *people like me*, are the only normal things about this place. Secondly, I don't gossip. That's woman's terrain."

Maggie drew in her breath sharply and she stomped a foot.

He noted this, amused. Willow's behaviour was making more and more sense. The apple, it seemed, hadn't fallen very far from the tree.

"Get out," she said. "Get out now before I call the police."

"Hey, be my guest, I'm sure they'd be interested in checking on the kid's welfare while they're here."

He'd gone too far. Willow was Maggie's pride and joy, the only thing she considered she'd ever got perfect in her life. She was proud of being a mother, and to have this man question her parenting made her furious. She walked over to the cupboard under the stairs.

"Where are you going?" he asked.

"To get my gun."

He didn't think she was serious. Not until she turned back around and he saw the gun in her hands. She's bluffing, he thought, amused. She probably doesn't have the first clue how to use it.

Then she cocked the rifle expertly and started loading it with ammunition.

"Whoa there, can we just back up a little?" he asked as he straightened up, holding out his hands in a gesture of peace. This was getting a little too serious. She didn't answer him, just carried on loading the gun.

'Look, I'm sorry if I offended you," he said placatingly, "that wasn't my intention."

Again, she didn't answer. She finished loading the gun and snapped it shut. Only then did she look back up at him.

"You still here?" she asked.

"Maggie -"

"Mrs Tanner."

"- Mrs Tanner, I'm sorry I upset you. I wasn't attacking your parenting skills, merely expressing my concern for the welfare of your daughter."

"My daughter is fine."

"If you say so."

"I do say so. Now leave before I use this thing. It hasn't been fired in awhile so although I may aim for your feet there's no telling which part of you I'll actually hit." She lifted her chin defiantly.

He stared at her, trying to judge if she was joking or not. She seemed serious so he decided he'd better not chance it. "Fine," he said, "I'll leave. I don't think you'd shoot but heck, you people are just crazy enough to prove me wrong." He turned to go but before he'd taken a step he quickly whirled around again. "You know, you should be grateful that I took the time to make sure your daughter was ok."

"Oh I am grateful for that. In case you've forgotten I even thanked you. Checking up on my daughter is *not* the reason I'm about to shoot you. Insulting her, me *and* this town, *is*. Now go, before I count to five. One, two, three..."

With one last studied look the man left. She heard his footsteps echo down the steps and then crunch off down the driveway. She unloaded the gun and put it back in the cupboard under the stairs.

Damn out-of-towners, she thought angrily. Coming to their little town and walking around thinking they were better than everyone else. She spied the piece of lake weed where she had dropped it on the kitchen table on her way to get the gun. Damn, she thought. It wasn't nearly enough for what she needed it for. That man had cost her one of her biggest sellers. Now what was she going to do?

Upstairs in the bath, submerged in water up to her chin and with steam curling the corners of the pages of her book, Willow thought of her jacket now lying at the bottom of the lake and smiled happily.

Chapter three

When Willow came downstairs again, fresh, scrubbed clean and pink from her bath, she immediately noticed the black cloud, consisting of her mother's cursed mutterings, hovering over the kitchen table. Her mother was busy at the oven, and she could smell a batch of fresh lavender soap cooking. Breakfast was on the table; fresh scrambled eggs from the hens out back, and bacon sourced from one of the farmers a few farms over.

"Has he gone?" she asked her mother.

"Yes."

"Good," Willow nodded. She opened the back door and gently shooed the black cloud outside. Then she went over to her mother and wrapped her arms around her mother's waist from behind.

"Sorry I didn't get enough weed," she said. Her mother's soaps were legendary in these parts, and her lake weed one was the most famous of all. Bathing with her lake weed soap attracted great prosperity, and more than one person in these parts owed their successes to her and her soaps.

Her mother twisted around in her grip and embraced her, kissing her on the top of her dandelion shampoo scented head.

"It's not your fault sweetheart. The only person to blame here is that horrible man. Who does he think he is? Questioning the way we live. As if I would *ever* let you do anything that put you in danger."

Then she crouched down a little until her eyes were on the same level as Willow's.

"All the same," she said, "I don't want you to go picking the weed by yourself anymore. Not because I don't trust you to be careful, I know you are. But I would die if anything happened to you, and that, *idiot,* has got me a little spooked. He made it sound like you nearly drowned out there."

Willow sighed. "I'm fine mum. You know I can hold my breath for ages."

"I know, but still, make sure one of us is with you from now on, just to make sure you're ok."

"If it'll make you feel better."

"It will. I love you so much kid."

"I love you too."

"Now eat," her mother said, gesturing towards the table. "Jugs boiling and then I'll whip us up a couple of hot chocolates. Your grandfather is nowhere to be seen so we can even have extra marshmallows without worrying about him scoffing the whole bag. Honestly, I wonder if anyone else has to hide sweets from their father if they want them to last longer than a day." She fetched the marshmallows from their hiding place at the back of the vegetable bin in the fridge. It was the one place Maggie could be sure her father would never look, knowing his aversion to anything green and leafy.

Willow sat down at the table and picked up the tall wooden pepper grinder.

"Where is he?" she asked, grinding pepper over the top of her eggs.

"God knows. There's been no sign of either of them this morning."

"I think Gran's gone bush," Willow said, her mouth full of delicious creamy eggs.

Her mother turned from stirring chocolate into a mug, frowning. "You're kidding."

"Nope, the whiskey's gone from the cabinet and her bed hasn't been slept in."

Her mother sighed. "Damn that woman. She was supposed to help me at the stall. She knows tonight is always my busiest night."

"I can help."

"Don't you have homework to do?"

"What makes you think I didn't do it already?"

"Have you?"

"Well, no. But that's not the point. I *could* have. You shouldn't make assumptions."

"But I was right though wasn't I. I wish you wouldn't always leave it to the last minute Willow. Why don't you do it Friday night and get it out of the way?"

Willow stared at her mother in horror. "Homework on a Friday night?" she said. "I can't think of anything worse. After a week stuck up in that stinky old classroom that's the last thing I feel like doing."

"I could help you."

"Oh yeah? What's the square root of 843?"

Her mother scrunched up her nose in thought. "Um," she said.

"That's what I thought," said Willow. "How about this, If Train A leaves its station at 7.42am and Train B leaves its station at 7.48am and they cross paths at 8.12am how fast is Train A travelling and what colour is the drivers gumboots?"

"Fine," her mother said, raising her hands in defeat. "Point taken. But your grandfather could probably help you, he used to be a real whizz kid at maths in his day."

"Please don't ever say whiz kid in front of any of my friends."

"You make me sound square."

"Please don't say 'square', in front of any of my friends either."

Her mother poked her tongue out at her. "Speaking of Nick, where is he? He normally arrives just in time for breakfast."

Willow scowled at her plate.

"We're not friends anymore."

"Oh dear. What happened this time?"

'I don't want to talk about it."

"Fine." Maggie got up and started to clear the plates. She knew her daughter and she knew she wouldn't be able to keep whatever was bugging her to herself for long. Sure enough,

"He said Sally 'Sookie' Jameson was, *pretty*!" Willow spat out the last word in disbelief. "What the hell is up with that?"

Maggie smiled, but facing the sink so her daughter wouldn't see.

"Don't say hell," she scolded mildly. "Is Sookie really her middle name?" she asked.

"Of course not. That's just our nickname for her. She squeals like a pig whenever anyone sees a spider in the class. Nick used to make fun of her too, but now he says she's pretty and he even walked her home two times last week. Noah said he saw them kissing outside her front door."

Maggie's eyebrows shot up. *What the hell?* "I guess you guys are growing up," she finally said. "He was bound to start becoming interested in girls sooner or later. Have you, you know, -?"

Willow frowned at her.

"Have I what?"

"- become curious about boys at all?"

"Gross! Don't be so disgusting."

Her mother walked over and kissed Willow on the head again. "I wish I could keep you this age forever," she said wistfully.

"Yeah well, you don't have to worry about me getting interested in boys anytime soon. I hate them."

They both turned at a sheepish cough from the back door that led off the kitchen.

"Morning Nick," Maggie said.

"Morning Mrs Tanner."

"Breakfast?"

"Only if you've got some going spare, thanks." He pulled out a seat and sat down.

'You've got some nerve showing up here," Willow said darkly. "Why aren't you having breakfast at your girlfriend Sally's house?"

"She's not my girlfriend."

"You finally see sense or did she dump your ass?"

"Willow," Maggie warned. "Stop cussing or I'll wash your mouth out with honeysuckle soap."

Washing with Maggie's honeysuckle soap left your skin feeling like it been kissed by the sun and massaged by the soft feet of bumblebees. However, a useful side effect had been discovered by parents, in that if used to wash a kids mouth out it left them unable to say a cross or nasty word about anyone or anything for a few days. Willow was still smarting from the last time her mother had carried through with the threat. She'd called her fellow classmates 'sweetie pie' and 'sugar cane' for days, even the ones like Sally Jameson who she couldn't stand. It had been a truly horrible experience and one she had no desire to repeat.

"Sorry mum."

She sat back in her chair and crossed her arms across her chest. She watched Nick as he devoured the food Maggie had placed in front of him.

"So what happened?" she asked him again. "Did she decide you're not good enough for her after all?"

"Something like that," Nick mumbled. He would never tell Willow the truth, that Sally had given him an ultimatum. It was either her, she announced, or Willow.

"You can't go out with me and still be friends with her," Sally declared, confident that he would make the right choice.

And he had. He'd given her a two finger salute and said, "Righto, see you round then," and walked away leaving her staring open mouthed after him. He'd pay for it, he knew. Sally would make his life a living hell for the next few weeks until a fresh victim caught her eye. But he had no regrets. Willow had been his best friend since he was six years old.

"What are you two planning on getting up to today?" Maggie asked them as she poured hot water into the sink in preparation for the breakfast dishes.

"That depends," Nick said with a mournful look at Willow. "Am I forgiven?"

She pretended to consider it. "Ok," she finally said. "I'll forgive you. But only if you do my homework."

She saw her mother's mouth start to open in protest.

"*Help* me do my homework, I meant to say. *Help*, not do." She grinned at her mother.

"I should think so."

"No problem," shrugged Nick. He'd already done his own on Friday afternoon, first thing when he got home. So he already knew the answers.

"If Nick helps me with my homework today, we can help you at the stall tonight, right?" Willow asked her mother.

"I guess so. But only if it's ok with Nick's mum."

"Yeah she won't mind," Nick said. "Where's Dot and Ray?"

Dot, short for Dorothy, and Ray, were Willow's grandparents. It was their house that Willow and Maggie lived in, and had done for most of Willow's ten and a half years.

Maggie scowled at the mention of her parents and the pan she was cleaning got a particularly vicious scrub.

"Dot's gone bush again, and as for Ray, your guess is as good as ours," said Willow.

"That woman acts like she's fourteen not seventy four," Maggie muttered. "Honestly" she turned and cupped her daughters face and traced the freckles on her nose with a finger tip, leaving a soapy bubble on the end, "if I end up as inconsiderate as her promise me you'll lock me away in an old folk's home or take me out back and shoot me. I don't want to be a burden."

"Ok," Willow agreed, rolling her eyes at Nick. It was something her mother had said to her many times.

"Right," Maggie placed the last plate onto the dish rack, dried her hands on a tea towel and checked her watch. "You two get cracking on that homework. I'm going to head into town to set up the stall for tonight. If I don't get there early enough I'll miss out on the best spots."

She took the soap out of the oven and left it on the windowsill to cool. The air in the kitchen took on the soft smell of lavender. Maggie's creamy lavender soap ensured the user a deep and peaceful slumber filled with wondrous dreams.

When her mother had left Willow spread her books over the kitchen table and sat back, kicking a table leg idly while

Nick sharpened a pencil. The scent of the soap started to make her feel drowsy and her eyelids drooped with heaviness.

"Wake up," Nick said, poking her with the now sharp tipped pencil.

"Ouch you idiot, that hurt." Willow rubbed at the small black mark on her arm where Nick had stabbed her. "You could have given me lead poisoning."

"Yeah right."

"You never know. You're going to feel pretty stink if I keel over and die."

"If you do can I have your bike?"

Willow kicked him under the table.

"No. Let's go outside," she said. "I'm falling asleep in here."

'What about your homework?"

"I'll do it later."

"We promised your mother we'd get it done."

"I don't remember making any such promise."

"Willow, she might ask and you know I can't lie to her. She has this way of knowing when I'm not telling the truth."

"Everyone in town knows when you're lying. Your ears go bright red and you bite your bottom lip."

"Aw hell, you might have mentioned this before you know. Might have saved me a bit of bother over the years."

Outside the day had warmed up. The sun was high and fat white fluffy clouds wafted slowly across the sky. It was like something from a kids drawing, except the sun wasn't an orange triangle with wavy lives in the corner. Dropping her school books in the grass, Willow and Nick lay flat on their backs under a big Magnolia tree and let dappled sun flicker across their skin.

"Can you believe we only have two weeks left of school?" Willow remarked, watching a fantail in the tree above scoot from branch to branch, chirping merrily all the while.

"I know, the end is in sight."

"Then we have two whole months of freedom," Willow said.

They both smiled in satisfaction at the thought.

From a distance they heard a car turn into the gravel road that led to Willow's driveway and Nick lifted himself up on to his elbows to look. Through the cloud of dust kicked up by the tyres he could just make out the shape of a red VW.

"Dot's home," he said, laying back down again.

The car turned into the driveway without slowing, and as it bumped up the potholed drive they could hear the song 'Ten Guitars' wafting out the open windows, along with a chorus of accompanying female voices. The car pulled to a stop in front of the house and Willow's grandmother climbed out of the backseat. She waved across at Willow and Nick and then went up the steps and into the house. Before she had disappeared the car was off again, rounding the top of the curved driveway where it paused briefly in front of Willow and Nick and three lined but beaming faces peered at them out of the window.

"Eh, Kia Ora Willow and Nick," Arihana said from the front passenger seat, her lined face creased up into a smile like a Sharpei dog.

"Hey Arihana, how was your night?"

"Oh choice dear, it was fabulous as always. You two behaving yourself?"

"Yes Arihana."

"Now that's disappointing," Arihana cackled, her voice throaty and husky from forty years of smoking Marlboro lights. "Your grandmother should have taught you better. Here," a dollar coin came flying out the window and bounced off Nick's right cheek.

"Ouch."

"Don't spend it all at once, you hear?"

"Yes Arihana."

Then the car took off back down the driveway, the stereo cranked up loud again.

They watched them leave. "Right," Willow sighed, rolling over and stretching out a fingertip to retrieve a book. "I suppose we better get this out of the way."

Chapter four

The centre of town was already a hive of activity when Maggie arrived. Representatives from the town council and volunteers were busy decorating the town square to give it a party atmosphere and construction workers were at work erecting a wooden stage at one end, from where a procession of local bands would provide entertainment that night.

It was a well attended event. Even farmers who rarely left the isolation of their properties made the effort, scrubbing up and driving in. It was a good excuse to meet up with distant neighbours and friends, share stories and catch up on any gossip. It was also a chance to support local produce and artists, and Maggie's soaps in particular were hugely popular.

As Maggie drove down Main Street looking for a park she spied Ray, camped out on the bench seat in the centre of town under the shade of a giant oak tree.

Back in the 1920's the townsfolk had planted some two hundred Oak trees, one to honour every local man from the area that had been killed during the war. Underneath each tree a cross was erected with the name and dates of the serviceman carved into its wood. Most of the oaks had flourished; growing straight and tall and proud, although over the years the odd one had succumbed to disease, lightning strikes and in one infamous incident, a lovers tiff, a bottle of Jack Daniels and an axe.

But amongst the young seedling trees there had been one that was smaller and spindly and with no leaves. It was basically one big stick with a few little sticks growing out of it. After careful deliberation it had been decided to plant that one on the village green and see what it would grow into. It would prove to be a portentous decision, as the tree had grown into an Angel Oak. Huge and gnarly and crooked, the branches of the tree curved and bowed and stretched out in all directions, some sagging right down to skim the ground. It was as if the tree had known from the time it was a sapling that its purpose was to grow and provide endless entertainment to children over the years, and as it grew it twisted and contorted itself into fascinating shapes.

Many a mother had left her children under the watchful eye of the tree while they did their shopping. The branches just itched to be climbed, and the mossy seats and leafy green undergrowth had fired up many an imagination. Over the years the tree had been used as a pirate ship and a castle. It had also served well as a witches hut, Peter Pan treehouse and a carriage, transporting many a princess to a ball or other such grand function. The trees uses were limited only to the imagination. A few years back someone had hung a few tyre swings from the lower branches, and the kids made full use of them.

The adults used it purely for shelter, although many of them could wistfully remember the fun they'd also had in the branches as children. The tree provided protection from the heat of the sun in summer, and in winter the thick canopy repelled the rain.

Permanent bench seats had been erected underneath, and now old men congregated there on weekends and any other day that also took their fancy, which were most days in summer. It was the best vantage point from where to observe the town's happenings.

Today, Ray had been joined by Sam, Henry and Alfred, (although everyone just called him Fred.) The men were musing over the opening of a new bakery shop when Maggie pulled up in front of them.

"Dad," she said, getting out of the car and addressing him over the roof, "did you take your pills this morning?"

"Yes I did," he said, "stop fussing."

"You can't blame me. Nine out of ten times you forget."

"Yeah well, today I remembered."

"Where's mum?"

Ray shrugged his shoulders. "She and the others went up bush. Probably be back sometime today. Nights are still too brisk for them to be gone for long."

At the mention of this the other men's ears perked up. Dot, Arihana, Hazel and Lois had been girlfriends since their young teens. Their friendship had withstood years of marriages, children, divorce, infidelity scandals and sickness. The women were as tight as knots in a rope and nothing had or ever could come between them, although over the years some had tried. Husbands, lovers and children had long resigned themselves to coming in second fiddle behind the friendship.

The four women were beauties in their time, envied and despised by some and admired and desired by others. They were a law unto themselves and refused to be dictated to by society. When others wore their hair prim and curled short around the ears like the queen, the four of them wore theirs loose and carefree around their shoulders. When the fashion called for wing tipped eyelids and dark stained lips, they wore nothing but a dusting of golden tan across their cheekbones and the sparkle of life in their eyes. Their lips curled knowingly with secrets only they knew. It infuriated the other women.

Every now and then the four of them left everything and took off up into the hills that rimmed the lake for a night or two. For years it had been a mystery as to what they were up to, and rumours swirled around lamp posts.

"They're up to no good," the towns' women sniffed piously some forty years previously. "What kind of a woman leaves her husband and children to fend for themselves while

36

they get up to god knows what in the hills. Mark our words, those girls are meddling in something dark, like witchcraft." This was meant to scare the men and curb their curiosity, but it had the opposite effect. Immediately their eyes glazed over as they pictured the women dancing naked under the moon.

Finally, one bright moonlit night back in the late fifties, a group of men had got wind that Dot and the others were planning on heading bush, and they banded together and told the wives they were headed to the lake for a spot of night fishing. Instead, they lay in wait under the ferns at the edge of the path that led up to the hills and when the four women passed by they followed them, from a distance by which they could still hear the women laughing but which they hoped would keep them unseen. The men were whipped into a fever of expectation; near quivering with the possibilities of the delights and wantonness they were to be privy to that night.

The quivering however, only kept them warm for so long, and after that they nearly froze to death out in the cold trees and undergrowth.

The women went into a large cave, the entrance to which was obscured from the casual eye by thick vegetation. Once inside they soon got a fire going, and from their hiding spot the men could only watch the flames dance merrily and long for the warmth they offered.

And that was it.

There was no nakedness, and no dancing.

To the men's immense disappointment not one single act of wanton behaviour took place.

There was only the clink as a bottle of whiskey was passed from woman to woman, the strumming of a guitar and the murmur of voices pierced by the occasional snort of laughter.

The men waited all night, trying to catch a glimpse of something, *anything,* that would make losing all sensation in their toes, (in some cases permanently,) worthwhile. But the next morning they headed home, disappointed and dejected, to face the fury of their wives.

For Dot, Hazel, Lois and Esme, their time in the cave was simply a chance to escape from the everyday struggles of life. Hazel's aunt Jemima had used the cave for the very same thing with her own girlfriends, and before she died she took Hazel and showed her where it was and told her to always remember that when your husband and children drive you to drink, a best friend will always be right there drinking alongside you. "A best friend," her aunt Jemima used to say, "will always be there for you, even when you've told them to get lost."

Dot and the others loved their husbands, for the most part. And they adored their children just as a mother should. But every woman needs an escape from it now and then, from the washing and the cooking and the constant background hum of "he started it! No *she* started it!" Every woman needs a chance to renew herself, and to reignite that spark inside of her that sometimes gets a little dimmed after everyday life gets in the way.

So every now and then when it all got on top of them, off they would go. And they would drink, and laugh, and share stories, and they would look out over the lake and remember that life stretched further than just the boundaries of this small town. It put things back into perspective.

And yes, there had even been, on occasion, a spot of nakedness. Sometimes when the whiskey had warmed the soul and spirits were high, they would run shrieking down to the lake and go skinny dipping under the iridescent moon.

The men just chose the wrong night to spy.

"Right, well if you see her," Maggie told her father, "remind her that she's supposed to be helping me set up the stall and running it tonight."

"Will do."

"And dad?"

"Yes?"

"Why don't you make yourself useful and help Willow out occasionally with her homework."

"The kid does homework?"

Maggie didn't bother answering him. On market days most of the car parks around town square, except for a precious few, were roped off, leaving plenty of room for the food stands and craft stalls and people to linger and talk. She had spied one of these precious car parks become available a mere twenty metres down the road and she quickly got back into the car and drove off to claim it. Just as she pulled up though, a black truck cut in from the other side of the road and stole the park.

"You've got to be kidding," Maggie said furiously. She double parked behind the truck and got out of her car, marching up to the driver's door and banging on the tinted window.

"Excuse me," she called out, "but this park is mine."

The door opened forcing her to take a step back and the glint of sun bouncing off the truck's bonnet momentarily blinded her. She heard a voice say, "show me where your name is and I'll let you have it."

She frowned, the voice was familiar.

"Don't be silly," she said. "You know that's not what I meant. I was clearly indicating to pull in here and you cut across and stole it, dangerously I might add."

"Well," the man behind the voice stepped out of the truck and smiled at her, "I didn't see you indicating. So I guess that makes the park mine. First in first served. It's only fair."

She sucked in her breath sharply. It was him, the man from this morning. The one who had questioned her parenting skills and insulted her town. The one she hoped had merely been passing through on his way to somewhere else.

"You," she said.

"Yep, me. How lovely to see you again, Maggie."

"Mrs Tanner."

"Still cross with me I take it."

"Are you deliberately trying to annoy me?"

"Of course not," he frowned. "Why on earth would I want to do that?"

"You tell me."

"You're awfully paranoid, aren't you."

A horn beeped out in the road and Maggie realised that she had caused a minor traffic jam to back up.

"Well, thanks to you I'm now running late," she said. "I hope you're happy," and she turned swiftly and hurried back to her car, ignoring the chuckle she heard over her shoulder.

"Happy?" she heard him say, "Of course I'm happy. That's twice in one day I've been lucky enough to run into you."

As Maggie drove off again cursing under her breath, Sam and the other men who had been watching the exchange with interest exchanged glances.

"Well well, I think it's fairly obvious what's going to happen there," Henry said, stretching out a leg that had started to go to sleep from sitting prone for so long.

"Yep," agreed Sam. "And it's about time too."

"What are you lot on about?" asked Ray.

"That man," Henry said, pointing with a shaky finger to where Jack was standing and watching Maggie as she drove off.

"What about him?"

"It's obvious he's taken a shine to your Maggie."

"Has he now?" Ray studied the man. He was tall and broad shouldered with long limbs. His hair was blond hair and it curled up at the nape of the man's neck - a touch too long in Ray's opinion. He couldn't see the man's face as he had his back to them, but he could tell from the admiring glances other women were giving the man and the way they pushed out their chests and fluffed up their hair that he must be what women considered good looking.

"It's been a heck of a long time since Jon left," Sam went on. "She's a beautiful girl. It's not right for her to be on her own."

"She's not on her own. She's got me and her mother and Willow."

"You know that's not what I meant. A woman like her deserves to be loved."

"Maybe so, but you know she's not about to start anything. She can't. Not with the way things are with Willow."

"You guys are still pulling that shit? Man that's crazy. That kid is old enough to know better. You underestimate her. Be straight up, she'll understand."

Ray held up his hands in agreement. "Hey it's not up to me, it's her mother's thing and I'm staying out of it."

They watched as Maggie appeared around a corner lugging two suitcases behind her. They could see that her expression was cross even from all the way across the square, and as she passed underneath trees the leaves shuddered and shrivelled away from her wrath.

Ray sighed and got to his feet, his knees creaking in protest like the branches on the ancient oak above him. "I'd better go help her," he said. "See you guys tonight."

Chapter five

With Ray's help Maggie managed to set her stand up in preparation for the night ahead in record time. There wasn't a great deal she could do in advance anyway, as she never put the soaps out until just before the market started. In the heat of the day they would start to soften and melt quickly, but once the sun went behind the big oak they would be ok. So it was simply a matter of setting up the tables. Three tables made up her little area, and she arranged them as usual in a U shape, with one in front of her and another on each side. The front table she covered with a pale lemon coloured cotton table cloth, the one on her right in mint green and the one on her left in rose pink. She loved colour, could never stand plain white anything. In fact, when she married Jon twelve years previously she had worn a dress made from dusky orange silk, with matching baby rose buds woven through her hair. It was quite out of the norm and hadn't been a popular choice with everyone who'd attended, but she and Jon had loved it and at the end of the day that was all that mattered.

Once the cloths were laid she opened the suitcases containing her stands. Ray carefully peeled off the layers of newspaper and passed them to her to arrange on the tables.

She fingered their cool surfaces lovingly as she placed them where she wanted them.

A few years back she'd grown tired of using wicker baskets to display her soaps in. The baskets gathered dust in the months between markets, and if it wasn't dust it was dirt from the garden after Dot 'borrowed' her baskets to go fruit or flower picking or to collect the eggs from the chickens. Maggie would have to scrub them clean every time she needed to use them, and over time the wicker had started to fray and fall apart and look messy.

By chance she had ducked into the second-hand shop one day to have a word to Mavis behind the counter about her goat breaking through the fence wires and raiding their vegetable garden again, and while there she had fallen in love on the spot with a vintage blue glass cake stand. It was gorgeous. Straight away she knew she had found a new way to display her soaps. She bought that stand and another one Mavis had, three tiered, ceramic with delicate flowers and birds and gold around the rim. And then every time she had a chance over the next few months she made trips to other second-hand and antique shops in other towns, and now she had an eclectic collection that was her pride and joy. Single story cake stands made from coloured glass and glazed ceramic, milk glass and even a couple made from Jadeite. She also had a big one made out of shiny tin, which she used to display her silver birch soap.

When rubbed into the joints the soap eased arthritis and muscular pain, so was in demand from the town's elderly and sportspeople.

No two were the same, and that's what she loved about them, the mismatch of it all. They displayed her soaps beautifully like they were cupcakes or some other such delectable treat, and few who passed by her stall could resist the temptation.

She had no issue with leaving her cake stands all set up as other stall owners were always around, as well as Ted, the overweight security guard pushing seventy who the council paid every market to wander around and keep an eye on things. Once she had everything where she wanted it she stepped out from behind the tables and surveyed it from the front, just as her customers would see it.

"Perfect," she declared. Then she checked her watch. "Just enough time to get home, shower and grab a bite to eat then be back here before it all kicks off."

"I'll see you at home," Ray said.

"Ok," Maggie agreed, blowing a kiss his way. "Wait, how'd you get into town this morning?"

Her father mumbled something under his breath, not quite able to meet her eye.

"Oh dad, tell me you didn't bring the bike? You know what Geoffrey said. Next time he sees you on it he's going to confiscate it, for good this time too."

"Honey, I've been driving that thing into town since long before Geoffrey's parents even held hands."

"Yes dad, I know. But he's the law and unfortunately what he says, goes. It's just not safe."

"Bullshit. I've never had an accident. Not once."

Maggie gave him a stern look.

"Ok once. But that truck wasn't looking where he was going. The accident had nothing to do with my driving."

Maggie sighed and rubbed one temple. "I don't have time for this. It's a farm bike dad, it's not meant to be on public roads. Drive it home now and then promise me you won't bring it into town again."

"Mm."

"*Promise me* dad."

"Fine," Ray stalked off. He was upset she knew, but he'd get over it. He valued his independence, always had done. And he was right; he *had* been riding farm bikes into town since before the roads round here were even tar-sealed. At least the one he drove now was a quad bike with four wheels, hence slightly safer than the old two wheeled one he used to own.

"I'll be back in about an hour," she called to Robert on the stand next to hers. He sold wooden carvings that he carved

47

himself from fallen trees on his and his neighbours' properties. As a self declared tree hugger, he refused to cut any tree down himself, but luckily the area was hit by enough storms and high winds in winter to ensure he had a steady supply of material.

"Sure," he called back to her. "I'll keep an eye on your tables for you."

"Thanks," she smiled at him gratefully. He was a nice guy, and they'd even gone for coffee once or twice but although he'd have loved for something more to happen, Maggie wasn't interested in things going any further. He wasn't her type for a start. She preferred her men masculine, not sandal wearing, beard growing hippies, nice as they may be.

She stewed as she made her way back to her car, remembering the earlier altercation with Jack. The man was a moron. Obviously where he'd come from that sort of behaviour was acceptable, but if he carried on like it here he'd soon find the townsfolk turning against him. His truck was still in the stolen park and she had to resist a childish urge to scratch a door. Instead she settled for kicking a tyre, a move that hurt her more than it did any damage to his truck.

"Dammit," she swore, hopping on one foot while her toes curled up in protest.

"Want me to fetch you some ice for that?"

Jack had come up behind her and was now leaning against a lamp post, watching her with obvious amusement. She felt her cheeks redden in embarrassment that he had caught her out in the act of behaving like a teenager, and she let her head drop so her hair covered most of her face.

"No thanks, I'm fine," she said.

"You sure? Looked like a pretty hard kick to me." His tone was cheeky, and she felt her anger return. She looked up at him and narrowed her eyes.

"You think you're pretty funny don't you."

He shrugged. "I've been told I have a great sense of humour, yes."

"Really? Well laugh at *this,*" and without even thinking about what she was about to do she kicked out her foot again, but this time at the car door, leaving a dent that was definitely going to require the services of a panel beater to remove.

Jack straightened up then. "What the hell?" he said, "I knew you were stroppy, but causing wilful damage to property?"

She stared in horror at the dent in the door. Why had she done that? She never let her temper get away from her. Here she was lecturing her father on obeying the law and then she turned around and did something like that? Thank god neither her father nor Willow had been around to see her juvenile behaviour. Gritting her teeth, she turned to Jack to apologise. But then she saw that he was laughing at her.

"You're an ass, anyone ever told you that?" she said furiously.

"Sure, every single one of my ex-girlfriends."

"Why don't you just do us all a favour and hurry up and get out of town. There can't be anything here that's possibly of any interest to someone like you."

He stopped laughing and regarded her, a dimple in his cheek puckered from the smile that still lurked just beneath the surface.

"Oh on the contrary," he said. "This town has something I'm fast becoming very interested in."

And even she wasn't naive enough not to catch the loaded innuendo behind the words. The way he looked her up and down when he said them left her in no doubt just what it was he was keen on.

"Not in a million years," she said, and with her cheeks burning she turned and quickly walked to her car. She half expected to hear footsteps behind her, at the very least asking for compensation for the damage she had caused, but he didn't follow. To her immense disappointment, this disappointed her.

All the way home she tried to avoid thinking about Jack. And all the way home, she failed. It had been a long time since she had verbally sparred with a man, and even though she couldn't stand *him*, she had enjoyed that part. In the six and a half years since Jon had left, she had focused purely on raising

Willow and on her soap business. It had gone from a hobby to something she'd had to get serious about in a hurry in order to pay the bills. She had no mortgage at least, not like others she knew who were struggling in these tough economic times. Her parent's house may have been in need of a lick of paint and a few new boards, but it was sturdy and it was freehold, and that was a huge relief.

However huge old houses like her parents weren't cheap to run, and then there were the other bills like chicken feed, school fees and new clothes for Willow who seemed to go through a growth spurt every other month. Her parents both drew a pension and they both contributed to household costs like food and electricity. But Maggie was proud and didn't want them to have to look after her and her daughter, so she had worked hard and over the years she had built her soap business up into a nice little earner. She sold a steady trade from home, to both locals and travellers passing by, thanks to a big sign that Willow and Nick had painted and hung from a large Pohutukawa tree on the main road. It was a simple sign, just wood with large blue letters, 'Homemade soaps made by Maggie Tanner - For Sale here!', and an arrow pointing down their road, but it had stall made Maggie cry a little with happiness the first time they showed it to her.

Her own little business of sorts. It was something she had dreamt of since she had been Willow's age and first discovered her knack for making soaps with medicinal and emotional benefits. The night markets were her biggest money earner; in one night she could make what sometimes took her a couple of months to earn otherwise.

Pulling up in front of the house she noticed the farm bike parked in the garage. Ray had beaten her home, which meant he must have either taken a short cut through Parker's farm or ignored the speed limit. She sighed. Perhaps her mother could talk some sense into him. Stepping inside the house she could smell something delicious frying; lamb chops if she wasn't mistaken.

"Mum?" she called out, stopping to strip off her T-shirt and throw it into the laundry beside the front door. She had worked up a sweat lugging the suitcases and setting up the tables and she only had a brief time in which to eat and freshen up. Wearing a black singlet and jeans she went into the kitchen where her mother was humming as she turned the chops over in the pan.

"Mum, where've you been? You were supposed to help me today, remember?"

Her mother pulled an apologetic face. "Sorry love, Hazel called last night all upset and I clean forgot."

Maggie sighed and opened the cupboard where the plates were kept to start setting the table. She was used to this sort of behaviour from her mother so couldn't muster up the energy to be really angry with her. There was no point. It was just how things were.

"She ok?"

"Who?"

"Hazel."

"Oh yes, she's fine now. Was just feeling a little upset and needed some time away. You know her husband Harry is in the early stages of dementia right, well yesterday he locked her out of the car at the supermarket and refused to let her back in. He called the police on his cell phone and told them she was trying to car jack him."

"Oh no, poor Hazel."

"Took the police two hours to talk him into unlocking the door."

"I hate to say it, but it sounds like Hazel needs help looking after him." Maggie lay out the cutlery and salt and pepper and stood back to see if she had missed anything. Sauce; her father refused to eat anything unless it had tomato sauce on it. She walked over to the fridge.

"She does, and that's what she realised yesterday. Her kids called from the city and told her she needs to put him in a specialty home, one where nurses can keep an eye on him properly. She needed to get away from it for awhile so got her brother and his next to useless wife in to babysit and she called me and the others. Mash those potatoes will you?"

"Mum," Maggie sighed, straining the boiled potatoes and adding a generous amount of butter and milk. "Why do you have to keep going to the cave? What's wrong with going out to a restaurant and having a nice meal together? Or inviting the girls around here and drinking yourselves drunk in the safety and warmth of your own home?" She bashed away at the spuds with the ancient stainless steel masher that had belonged to her own grandmother. The thing was bent out of shape from years of use but still served its purpose.

Her mother shook her head dismissively. "You could never understand," she said. 'It's just something we do. We've always done it." She turned the element off on the stove and started piling the brown and crispy chops onto a platter.

"Just because you've always done it doesn't mean it makes any sense. You guys aren't getting any younger. I worry about you."

"Get the salad out of the fridge please," her mother said, changing the subject in a way that clearly meant the conversation was finished.

Maggie did so. Then she walked over to the lounge where her father was sprawled out on the couch while Baywatch repeats played on the TV. His eyes were closed and he was snoring gently. He looked peaceful. She picked up the remote and pushed the button to turn the TV off.

"Hey I was watching that," her father protested, wiping away some dribble that had collected in the corner of his mouth.

"With your eyes closed?"

"A moments rest."

"Dad, you've seen those shows a hundred times." Her father loved Baywatch so much and was so upset when the show finished that Dot had bought him every season's box set on video. He had played them so many times the ribbons were wearing thin and the spools creaked every time he pressed play. It was only a matter of time before they started falling apart.

"Not my fault they only put crap on TV these days."

"Willow, dinner's ready," Maggie called up the stairs on her way back to the kitchen. She heard her daughters feet hit the floor above and then thunder down the stairs, taking them two at a time. She bounced into the kitchen and put her arms briefly around her mother before dragging out her chair and sitting down.

"Lift it, don't scrape it," Ray said, as he said every night and which Willow took no notice of.

"You're in a good mood," Maggie appraised her daughter.

"That's because summer is nearly here. And because I'm looking forward to the market tonight."

"Did you finish your homework?"

"Yep."

"All of it?"

"Yep."

"And how much of it did you do, and how much did Nick do?"

"I'd say about fifty-fifty."

"Willow, how will you ever learn if Nick does all your work for you?"

"I don't *need* to learn Math's. That's what calculators are for. And what am I ever going to use science for when I'm a grown up? Do you use science in your everyday life?"

"Can't say that I do," Ray commented, squeezing the sauce bottle upside down and covering his chops and potatoes with a generous amount.

"Besides, you know I'm going to be a writer," Willow went on, "so really English is the only subject worth paying any attention too."

"She has a point," Dot said.

"Will you two stay out of it please?"

"School never did me any favours," Ray ignored her.

"Shut up dad."

"I'm just saying, it's not the be all and end all of life. She's a bright kid, she has other options."

"Oh crap, look at the time," Maggie shoved the last forkful of salad in her mouth and pushed her chair back.

"Lift it, don't scrape it," her father said.

"And don't swear in front of Willow," her mother added.

"Give me ten minutes to shower and change and then whoever wants to come better be ready and waiting at the car. Anyone who's not will be left behind."

Twelve minutes later she emerged from the house, refreshed and in a clean long navy and white striped dress. She stopped short. None of her family were anywhere in sight. She threw up her hands.

"Oh for the love of -," she said but was cut off by giggling.

"Very funny you lot," she called. "Now hurry up."

Ray, Dot and Willow emerged from around the side of the house.

"Told you she'd freak out," Willow said satisfactorily.

"I did *not* freak out, but you all get in the car *now* before I do."

Chapter six

The decorators had done a wonderful job since Maggie had been gone and the centre of town now looked like something from a fairytale when the family arrived. They'd parked a few streets back and walked the rest of the way, each of them carrying a backpack or suitcase containing Maggie's soaps. As they made their way they passed neighbours and friends, all heading the same way, and all greeted each other enthusiastically like long lost friends.

Colourful Chinese lanterns, lit from inside with tea light candles, were hanging from the oak and strings of fairy lights had been woven around its branches. As well as the Oak in the centre, large rhododendron trees framed the square. They had just started to drop their flower and the ground was carpeted in a deep layer of pink and red flowers. Young girls were prancing amongst them and throwing the flowers over each other's heads. The petals fell like confetti, and the girls giggled and pretended they were attending each other's weddings. Alf Parker and Hemi Akurangi had both filled the back of their trucks with square hay bales and brought them into town, and now there was a nice seating area set up in front of the stage where a band had already started playing.

Energy and anticipation were thick in the air, and excitement jumped from person to person until before long the whole square was filled with tapping feet, humming throats and bobbing heads. Wallets were fished out of back pockets where they had dwelt since the last market and were dusted off. Before long there were queues at all the food stands. There was quite an ethnic selection; Indian kebabs and curries, Maori Rewena bread, Paua and Whitebait fritters, Italian ciabatta sandwiches heavily loaded with sundried tomatoes and feta cheese and drizzled with extra virgin olive oil. The combined smell was simply heavenly, and it drifted on air currents, tickling noses and tiptoeing across taste buds.

Maggie made her way through the people to her stall.

"Hey," Robert called. "Quite a few people have been looking for you already."

"I hope I haven't missed any sales," Maggie worried.

"Don't worry, they'll be back," Ray said, dumping his bag of soaps on the ground behind the stall and looking around for his friends. They were easy enough to spot as they were camped out on the same bench seat as earlier in the day, in the same positions even. If it wasn't for their combed hair and clean shirts he would have thought the guys hadn't even been home. No one else dared sit there; it was an unspoken town rule that the seat belonged to the old men. "I'll see you lot later," he said, kissing his wife on her cheek and ruffling Willow's hair.

"Get off," she said, ducking out of reach.

Dot and Willow helped Maggie unpack the soaps and arrange them on the cake stands. With the three of them working hard it only took a matter of ten minutes. Once finished they stepped back and admired their handiwork. The colourful soaps looked enticing, and in the early evening heat their oils started to release their smell and soon the air around the stand was hazy and filled with tantalizing aromas.

Immediately people started drifting towards the table, and for the next hour Maggie served people, one after the other, listening to their needs and then matching them to the appropriate soap, while Dot handled the money and Willow bagged up the purchases.

"See," her mother said to her at one point, "Math's can be useful in some situations."

Willow rolled her eyes.

After an hour the steady line turned into a trickle and for the first time Maggie had a chance to look around.

"The place looks amazing," she said proudly.

"Hmm," Dot agreed.

Willow had been eyeing up the ice cream truck for the last hour, and she finally saw her chance.

"Darling mother who I love very much," she said.

"Ok what are you after and how much is going to cost me?"

"How do you know I'm after something?"

"Because you only act super sweet like this when you're after something."

"It upsets me that you would think such a thing mother," Willow pouted.

But Maggie knew her daughter better than that. "Well?" she said. "I'm waiting."

"Fine. Can I have an ice cream?"

"What's the magic word?" her grandmother asked.

"Abracadabra."

Dot threw back her head and roared with laughter.

"Don't encourage her," Maggie said to her mother.

"Encourage what? She's sassy, it's a good character trait to have."

"Well we all know where she gets it from, don't we."

"There's nothing wrong with a little bit of sass," Dot shrugged. "Better to have a kid with some spark then a wet blanket like Lois's granddaughter. Now *that* kid needs a personality transplant."

"Mum," Maggie frowned, "don't say things like that in front of Willow."

"Why not?"

"Because she'll go to school and repeat it, that's why not. I got a phone call the other week from her principal complaining that Willow told the whole class that the teacher was an impotent fool. Now where do you think she heard that?"

Dot had the good grace to look guilty.

"Oh," she said. "Right. Yes I may have said something along those lines. But in my defence I was talking to Ray, not Willow."

"You see these things?" Maggie grabbed one of Willows ears in each hand and gave them a wiggle. "They're called ears. And they're always listening."

Dot regarded her granddaughter, who was openly enjoying seeing her grandmother in trouble for once instead of her. "You did it on purpose didn't you, knowing it would get back to your mother." she guessed shrewdly.

Willow shrugged. "Hey I'm just a kid. You're the adult who really should know better."

"Well played," Dot nodded admiringly, "well played indeed. Here," she thrust a hand inside her shirt and rummaged around inside her bra, pulling out a ten dollar note. Dot didn't believe in carting around a purse. If she couldn't fit it in a pocket or in her bra then she didn't need it. She passed the warm and slightly damp note over to a cringing Willow. "Get yourself an ice cream, and get me a chocolate cone too. You want one?" she asked this last question to Maggie.

"You know what, it's so warm tonight I think I will. A strawberry one please."

While Willow was gone and the stall was having a quiet lull, Maggie took the opportunity to tidy up the soaps, putting ones that had been mixed up back in the right place and seeing which ones needed restocking. She was almost all out of her Kowhai soap she noticed with surprise. The soap was made from the yellow flowers of the native tree, and was useful for when the bather was going through a crisis. It couldn't give any answers, but it helped soothe and wash troubles and anxiety away, at least so a good night's sleep could be had.

She was underneath the table, rummaging to find which bag she had more in when she heard a now familiar voice.

"Excuse me," she heard Jack say to her mother. "But I was told I'd be able to find Maggie Tanner here?"

Maggie crawled as far under the table as she could, shaking her head up at her mother and mouthing the word, "Noooooo," as clearly as she could.

"That depends," Dot answered him.

"On what?"

"On who's asking."

Jack held out a hand. "My name is Jack. I'm a friend of Maggie's."

Underneath the table Maggies' mouth dropped open. Friend? The man was more arrogant than she had first suspected.

"Pleasure to meet you Jack, I'm Maggie's mother, Dot," said Dot, taking the hand and admiring his long fingers. "You know, I thought I knew all of Maggie's friends, but I've never heard mention of you before."

"It's a fairly, *recent,* friendship. Lovely to meet you too Dot. Wow, I can see where Maggie gets her good looks from."

Dot preened. He was smooth, she'd give him that. It made a welcome change from some of the farmers around here who barely knew how to talk to a woman, let alone woo one.

"Seems to me Maggie might have mentioned someone as good looking as you," she cooed flirtatiously, and then flinched and swore as her ankle was slapped hard from underneath the table. Jack heard the sound of the slap and smiled.

"Maggie's stepped away for a moment," Dot told Jack. "But I can pass on a message if you like."

"Sure thanks, that'd be great. Can you let her know that I'll get the bill for the damage to the truck tomorrow, but we can discuss that over dinner. I'll pick her up around seven. Tell her to wear something sexy."

That was it. Maggie went to stand up, outraged, but in her hurry she failed to back out far enough and smacked her head on the underside of the table as she got up.

"Son of a bitch," she swore, rubbing it.

"Don't swear," said Dot.

64

"Maggie," Jack said in fake surprise. "Excuse me," he said, and leant forward over the table to peer down.

"What are you looking for?" Maggie asked him irritably.

"Just checking if there's anyone else hiding down there."

"I wasn't *hiding*, for your information. I was getting more soap."

He looked pointedly at her empty hands.

"You interrupted me."

"Right. I was just telling your mother that I'll pick you up at seven tomorrow. For dinner. Wear something nice."

"I heard. And obviously I wasn't clear enough this afternoon when I said *not in a million years*. So let me see if I can spell it out a little clearer. I'm not interested. You are annoying, rude and arrogant, and I wouldn't date you if you were the only man left alive."

"Phew," Jack whistled through his teeth. "Say what you really think why don't you. Don't hold back out of any concern for my feelings."

"Feelings? I doubt you understand the meaning of the word. You insulted my parenting and my home today and that showed zero concern for *my* feelings."

"That was a misunderstanding, and if you crawled out of your own butt for a second and looked at it from my point of view you would appreciate the fact that I was only expressing my concern."

"See that's exactly what I'm talking about. Rude. You just proved my point one hundred percent."

He sighed and held up his hands in a conciliatory gesture. "I'm sorry, again. Look, how about we start afresh. Pretend today never happened, and get to know each other properly."

"Like I said, I'm not interested. Besides, I think my husband might have something to say about it."

She heard Dot start to say something beside her and kicked out, connecting with an ankle again.

"Ouch. Will you please stop doing that?"

Maggie ignored her and stared at Jack defiantly. He held her gaze longer than was polite, his eyes roaming over her face. She could see something in his eyes that she hadn't seen from a man in a long time, and it both thrilled and terrified her.

"My apologies," he finally said. "I was led to believe you were single and available."

"You were given the wrong information. I'm married." She tucked her hand behind her so he wouldn't see the lack of a ring.

"My apologies again," he said, but she could tell from the questioning tilt to his head that he knew she wasn't telling him the entire story.

"Oh great, it's you." Willow was back with the ice creams. She frowned at Jack. "What do you want?"

"Willow, don't be rude," Maggie said, despite the fact that the statement made her a hypocrite. She took the strawberry cone that Willow passed her. Her daughter had lingered and detoured on her way back, and the ice cream had started to succumb to the heat that still shimmered in the air. Ribbons of melted ice cream were making their way down the sides of the cone and on to her hand. Without thinking she licked them off, and blushed when she saw Jack watching her.

"What are you still doing here?" she snapped, embarrassed that her body had reacted without her control. "Go away, you're blocking potential customers."

He turned and looked over his left shoulder, then his right. There was no one behind him. Making his point without a word, he turned back to her.

"Fine," he said. "I'll leave you to it. Lovely to meet you Dot, and as always a pleasure to see you, Willow." And with one last smile flicked at Maggie he left. Her eyes followed him until she realised the other two were regarding her with interest.

"What?" she asked defensively.

"Anything you'd care to tell me?" Dot asked.

"No."

"What did he mean by 'damage to his truck'?"

"It's nothing, drop it."

67

"Didn't sound like nothing," Dot said, but she let it go because Willow was watching them. She fully intended on raising the subject later with Maggie, but for now she sat in a deck chair and enjoyed her ice cream.

"I'm going to the bathroom," Maggie annouced heading out from behind the stall. She didn't add that she needed to splash some cold water on her still burning cheeks.

"How very interesting," Dot mused, watching her daughter make her way through the throngs of people enjoying the evening. "It's fairly obvious what's going to happen there, if you ask me."

"What?" asked Willow.

"What's what?" Dot jumped in her chair, she had forgotten that her granddaughter was listening.

"You said it's obvious what's going to happen there - what's going to happen?"

"You shouldn't sneak up on people. It's nothing you need to worry about."

Willow sighed. "I didn't sneak up on anyone. I was standing right here the whole time. Maybe you should actually wear your glasses for a change."

"Wash your mouth out," Dot reached out a hand to smack playfully at Willow. Aging and its bag of side effects was a touchy subject with Dot. She preferred to ignore it and pretend it wasn't happening.

"Hey," said Nick, who had arrived at the stall and was standing there looking nonchalant, as if he hadn't just turned up hours too late to help out.

"Where've you been?" Willow demanded.

He shrugged. "Around. I came by earlier but you guys were packed. Didn't seem to need me so I went and ate some food and watched the bands."

"Typical."

"So are you done?"

Willow turned to her grandmother, smiling sweetly. "Grandmother darling, you know how much I love you, right?"

"Go," Dot laughed. "But be back in an hour. I'll square it with your mother."

"Thanks Gran," Willow kissed her quickly on the cheek, after making sure no one from school was around to notice, then she took off with Nick.

Dot watched her go and her expression turned serious. The kid was growing up. She wouldn't be as easy to fool anymore. If Dot had her way they would have come clean to her years ago, but Maggie had stuck to her guns in a misguided effort to protect her daughter. Dot wondered if the arrival of Jack in their lives was going to change anything. He certainly didn't seem the type to give up easily.

Ah well, she thought. Only time would tell.

Chapter seven

"So what's for dinner tonight?"

This innocent question was not typically a question most mothers would ask their young daughter on a Sunday morning. But then this had never claimed to be a typical household.

"Dunno, just on my way out to check now."

When Willow was out the front door and far enough out of earshot Ray, who was sitting at the kitchen table, lowered his newspaper and gave Maggie 'a look'. He had finished his porridge and was loitering over coffee and the paper.

"What?" she asked.

"You know what. How much longer are you going to keep this up?"

"Now is not the time to discuss it dad."

"Your mother and I think you need to be straight with her."

"Seriously dad, leave it. So what's it to be?" Maggie asked the last bit loudly as Willow re-entered the house. "Personally I'm hoping for chicken. We haven't had one of those for awhile, have we dad?" Her tone warned her father to play along.

"No," Ray sighed. "We haven't." He lifted the paper back up in front of his face.

"Sorry mum, looks like Lamb," said Willow carrying the large cut of meat in a plastic bag gingerly in front of her. "Yuck, all the blood is dripping out of a hole in one corner."

"Quick pass it here then," Maggie opened the oven drawer and pulled out a roasting pan. She held it out and Willow dropped the meat inside with a thud then walked to the sink to wash her hands.

"It's a big one alright," Maggie commented. "It'll be delicious slow roasted with some rosemary and garlic."

Willow finished washing her hands and then walked to the fridge to get juice. She stood there with the door open, perusing the contents.

Maggie frowned, watching her. Willow didn't seem too enthused by the roast, and as much as she was loath to admit it, maybe her parents were right? Her little white lie all those years ago had snowballed and now she had absolutely no idea how she was supposed to come clean, although she knew she would have to eventually. One day Willow was going to start asking more questions.

Dot came banging through the back door with an empty washing basket in her hands.

"Those towels will be dry in about ten minutes I reckon," she said. "That's some breeze kicking up out there. It's lovely though, I can smell summer lurking just around the corner."

"Oh yeah?" said Willow, sitting down at the table with her juice. "And what does Summer smell like exactly?"

"You don't know? And you call yourself a writer? My girl, use your imagination." Dot stood behind Willow and placed her hands on her shoulders. "Close your eyes," she told her. "Right I'll start. Summer to me smells like cut grass, and hot tar seal. It smells like the pollen of freesias, jasmine and lilacs, honeysuckle and sweet peas, mixed with the stench of cow manure from the farms of course," she laughed when Willow screwed her face up. "Now *you* think, what does summer smell like to you?"

Willow thought of hot summer days. "Coconut scented sun tan lotion," she finally said, "and chlorine in my hair from the pool at school."

"Good," her grandmother nodded. "Very good."

Ray lent back in his seat. "For me, summer smells of sausages, steaks and corn cobs grilling and sizzling on the BBQ."

"A freshly sliced watermelon," Maggie joined in as she finished scrambling some eggs and slid them on to a plate which she put down in front of her daughter.

"Clean and crisp sheets that have been hanging in the sun all day," said Dot.

They all started adding new ones as they thought of them.

"That sulphuric smell in the air just before a thunderstorm, and the clean smell of the concrete after summer rain."

"The smell a tomato plant makes when you brush up against it."

"Citronella candles to scare the mossies away on hot nights."

"Fresh mint ice tea."

"Strawberries warm from the sun."

"The smell of water when it comes out of a hose that has been lying on the lawn all day in the sun."

"Sweat from thirty kids cooped up in a classroom."

"That's disgusting Willow."

"Tell me about it."

"I remember the hot sweet smell of my mother canning fruit," Dot said wistfully.

"My dad's cigarette smoke as he tinkered with something out in the garage, doing his darnedest to stay out of my mother's way," said Ray.

"Algae from when the lake overflows and then drains away, leaving pockets of water behind that turn stagnant," Willow said.

Her family stared at her.

"What?" she asked defensively.

"That was a lovely description," her mother said, kissing her on the top of her head. "You are going to be a wonderful writer one day."

"Well thankfully we don't have long to wait before we can smell all that again," Dot said as she picked the basket up from the table where she had rested it while she reminisced. "What's for dinner?" she asked, as she headed past them towards the laundry.

"Lamb."

"Delicious."

Willow finished off her eggs and pushed back her chair.

"Lift it, don't scrape it."

"Mum, can I go meet Nick now?"

"Ok. You two got something planned?"

"Fishing."

"In the lake?"

"Creek."

"Bring me home trout this big for the smoker," said Ray, extending his hands as wide as he could to either side of him.

"I'll try my hardest."

Willow left the kitchen and about five seconds later they heard her scream, "Nooooo." They both jumped to their feet and ran to the front door.

"What is it, what's wrong?" Maggie called out, her heart all the way up in her mouth from the sound of her daughter in trouble. She stopped at the top of the steps when she saw her daughter standing in the drive, still in one piece and, as far as Maggie could tell, unscathed. Then Maggie saw what had made Willow howl the way she had.

"You again."

"Morning," Jack said cheerfully. He was holding out something made of pink plastic, with large comical strawberry faces plastered all over it. Willow's raincoat. Willow herself had backed away and was staring at him as if had come bearing a human head on a stick.

"Where the hell did you find that?" she asked in disbelief.

"Willow, don't swear."

"But...the last time I saw *that thing* was at the bottom of the lake. *Weighed down with stones*. I thought I'd finally got rid of it." She saw her mother's face and hurriedly added, "I mean, I was really worried that I'd never see it again."

"Anyone would think you tried to lose it on purpose," said Dot as she emerged from the house to see what all the noise was about.

"Well duh, of course I did."

"*Willow*," Maggie warned.

"Sorry," Willow muttered darkly, not looking sorry at all.

"Where did you find it?" Maggie reached out to take the coat off Jack.

"Washed up on the shore of the lake," he said. "Rufus and I were out taking our morning walk. He led me down a path and there it was, washed up on the shore, none the worse for wear."

Willow scowled at Rufus who had the decency to look mournful. "Stupid dog. You couldn't have just kept on walking, could you?"

Maggie turned the coat over in her hands. He was right, it was in remarkably good condition considering it had spent the night at the bottom of a lake. No rips or tears; it was as shiny as the day Dot had first brought it home.

"Thank you for bringing it back," she said to Jack, then turned to go back inside the house. She hoped he would take the hint and leave.

"Rufus," her dad piped up. "That's a terrible name for a dog."

Jack sighed. "So people keep telling me."

"I told him he should have called it Apollo," said Willow.

"Now *that's* a name a dog can be proud of," agreed Ray. "That, or Shadow," he mused. "I've always thought if I had a black dog that's what I'd call it."

"Lucky we never got one then," said Willow.

"Don't be so bloody cheeky."

"Don't swear," said Dot and Maggie.

Jack looked from face to face in amusement. Then he looked over Maggie's shoulder at the big old house behind her.

"What an amazing house," he said. "I'd love to see inside."

Maggie's mouth dropped open at his audacity, which was a shame because she was too slow to close it again and answer, so her father got in first.

"Come on in lad, I'll give you a tour." Ray was very proud of the house he'd worked hard to buy and had owned for almost fifty years.

Collecting herself, Maggie smiled a warning at Jack behind her father's back.

"I'm sure Jack has other places to be and other people to annoy," she said.

"Nope," Jack said, "just here and just you."

Then he swept passed her with a grin and followed Ray up the porch steps and into the house.

Maggie watched him go, dumbfounded at this sudden turn in events.

"You'll catch flies," remarked Willow.

Maggie snapped her mouth shut.

Rufus gave a little whine and looked up at them woefully out of his big brown eyes. His ears drooped and he gave a heavy sigh.

"I'll just stay here and look after your dog shall I?" Maggie yelled after Jack.

Jack's head appeared back in the doorway. "Oh he'll be fine," he said. "He won't go anywhere."

"Can I take him fishing with me?" Willow asked.

"No," said Maggie.

"Sure," said Jack at the same time.

"She'll be gone for hours."

"I don't mind hanging out here until she's back. That is, if it's ok with you?"

"No, it's not."

"Of course it is, you can stay for lunch," said Dot, at the same time.

"Know anything about quad bikes?" Ray, who had appeared back in the doorway beside Jack to see what the holdup was, asked. "It's started making a funny clunking noise."

"Not a thing," Jack said, "but I'll take a look."

'I'll whip us up some cheese scones and a quiche," decided Dot. "And maybe a cake if there's time."

"Have you lot lost your mind?" asked Maggie. "We know nothing about this man."

Her parents frowned at her.

"That doesn't mean we can't extend our hospitality," said Dot.

"Don't be so rude," Ray said to Maggie. Then he turned to Jack. "Sorry about that," he said, "we raised her with better manners but the older she gets the more she seems to forget them."

"*Dad.*"

"What? It's true."

"You guys are weird. I'm off," said Willow. She slapped her hand on her thigh and whistled at Rufus, who looked to Jack for consent.

"Off you go," he gave it.

The dog seemed reluctant but nevertheless he trotted over to Willow's side and headed off with her down the driveway.

"Be careful," Maggie called.

"Don't forget to catch me a big one," Ray called.

Willow waved back over her shoulder. "Yeah, yeah."

"I don't know what you two are playing at but you can just it stop right now," Maggie frowned, turning to where her mother had been standing twenty seconds before. She was gone, and Jack and her father had disappeared back inside the house. She was alone in the driveway talking to herself. She kicked a pebble viciously then flinched as it bounced off the front of the house, narrowly missing a window.

"I've got to stop kicking things," she sighed to herself, heading into the house. She dumped the coat in the laundry to be washed later. There was no sign of her father or Jack, but her mother was in the kitchen measuring flour out onto a pair of old green kitchen scales and humming happily to herself.

"Can I add some hemlock to that mixture?" muttered Maggie, grabbing an apple from the bowl on the table and leaving without waiting for her mother to answer. She headed to the room she had transformed into her little shop at the back of the house. As well as the internal entry it had its own external door, so that customers didn't traipse through the house. Opening the door she stepped inside and closed it behind her, and immediately she felt some of the tension leave her shoulders. She took a deep breath and shook her arms out, twinkling her fingers, shaking the stress from her body.

"Much better," she said then she took a big bite from her apple, enjoying the loud sound of the crunch echoing in the quiet solitude of her room. She walked over to the small stereo in one corner and flicked the on switch. It was set to the local radio station, to Willow's disgust, as, according to her, it played a selection of 'ancient' and 'uncool' songs. However Maggie enjoyed them, and humming along to the one that was currently playing she walked over to the tall bench she used as her counter. It came up to just above her waist and was heavy, solid wood. She'd found it dumped in a skip outside someone's house, and had became its proud owner after knocking on the front door and asking if she could have it. Sanded down and given a few coats of varnish, it had come up looking like she'd paid thousands of dollars for it. The bags with the unsold soaps from last night's markets were on the counter and she started to unpack them, stopping only every now and then to take more bites from her apple.

She was so engrossed in what she was doing that she didn't hear the door open, and it was only when she turned around and bumped into him that she realised Jack had entered the room.

"What are you doing in here?" she asked taking a step back, frowning at him for invading her space.

"I'm lost, sorry. I was looking for the bathroom but I must have misheard your father's directions." His eyes scanned the room and its contents. He wandered over towards one of the shelves and started reading the framed cards with pictures of each different kind of soap and explaining what its benefits were.

"What exactly did my father say?"

"He said, 'up the stairs and last door on the far right. You can't miss it'."

"Oh I see. This is you being funny again is it?"

"I don't know what you mean."

"This room, as you well know, is on the ground floor and is at the back *left* of the house."

"Ah. My mistake. He obviously meant *the other right,*" Jack grinned.

"Idiot."

"Now that's just not nice. Your father's right, your manners do leave a lot to be desired." He turned back to the soaps.

Speechless, Maggie resorted to poking out her tongue and stomping a foot hard on the floor. Unfortunately he turned at just that moment, catching her.

"You know," he said, "you do like to express yourself in a most interesting way."

"Shut up."

"No I'm serious. It's rather fascinating."

"Well I find you insanely annoying and I wish you hadn't come here. In fact why are you here? Wasn't I clear enough last night?"

"Oh perfectly clear. I came to return your daughters raincoat, remember?"

"But why are you *still* here? I told you, I'm not interested in going out with you. Not to dinner or anywhere else."

"I know. And don't worry, I'm not interested in going out to dinner with you anymore either."

Maggie narrowed her eyes at him, suspecting another joke.

"You're not?"

"Nope."

"You're not here to try and get me to agree to go out with you?"

"Nope."

"But, yesterday, and last night - you were so insistent."

"That was then. I've moved on now."

She crossed her arms and leant back against the counter. "You've moved on."

"Yep."

"Fickle aren't you?"

"Hey, I know when a man's beat. I'm no sucker for punishment."

He had picked up one of the cards and was studying it closely.

Maggie couldn't understand why this change in attitude left her feeling a little deflated. It wasn't that she liked the man, quite the opposite. She could only guess it was because for the first time in a long time she had felt wanted. She had enjoyed the thrill of being chased, albeit briefly. It was just a shame she hadn't enjoyed the person doing the chasing.

"Well that's good," she said. "I'm glad you finally got it through your thick skull."

"Ouch, I'm glad too. My ego couldn't take your compliments."

She walked over to the door and opened it, standing to one side.

"I have work to do," she said, in a clear sign of dismissal.

"I'll leave you to it then," he walked over and stood a little too close than was polite. His eyes looked into hers like he was trying to read the instructions stamped on her heart, and she could feel his breath, hot on her face. It made all the little hairs on her arms stand up and tingle. She shivered.

He noticed.

"Here," he said softly, and she felt parts of her body that had been dormant start to awaken. He pressed something into her hands, and the shock of his fingers touching hers caused her to gasp as if she had just submerged herself into a cold creek on a hot day. He smiled and left, and she slammed the door closed behind him and kicked it, despite her earlier promise. It took a minute for her breathing to slow and her heart to beat at its normal rate. She looked down at what he had given her; it was one of her soaps, creamy white with purple flecks. She sniffed it. Lilac. Even though she knew exactly what it would say she crossed the room and picked up the card he had been reading.

'Purple Lilac – widely considered to be a harbinger of spring. If you are experiencing the first flushes of a love affair, bathe with this beautiful soap and it will greatly enhance your exhilarating and beautiful new emotions. Be warned though, you will be unable to contain yourself from declaring your new love, so use only if a declaration is considered appropriate'

What the hell was he playing at? She put the soap back where it had come from, but not before smelling it again. As well as the lilac there was a trace of something else; his scent still lingered, she realised. It hinted at sandalwood and mint, earthy and woody tones.

"First flushes of a love affair my ass," she muttered. "One second he says he's moved then the next he's giving me soap with a meaning like that? Stupid man. Makes no sense."

She carried on muttering along the same lines as she attempted to go back to unpacking the soaps, but when she realised that she was mixing them all up, she threw her hands up in frustration.

"Damn him," she said, knowing it was Jack that had left her so flustered.

"Well I guess there's no point trying to work today," she decided, and she switched off the radio and left the room. She was hoping to avoid everyone but as she walked through to the living/dining/kitchen area her parents and Jack were all there, seated around the table and chatting as if old friends. Her mother really wanted to impress, Maggie noted. The table was set with a jaunty red and white checker tablecloth and bowls of fresh whipped cream and saucers of jam adorned the top, as did matching plates and cutlery. Maggie briefly wondered how her mother had managed to find a matching set; the drawers and cupboards in this house were so stuffed full with an assortment of crockery and cutlery acquired over the years that it was rare to find two pieces the same.

"Darling," her mother said, oven mitts protecting her hands as she held a tray of hot, steaming scones straight from the oven. "I was just about to come and fetch you."

"Thanks, but I'm going out," Maggie answered, grabbing her keys from the hook by the front door.

"I thought we would all have a nice lunch together, get to know our guest a little better" her mother said, raising her eyebrows and nodding sideways towards Jack.

"I'm pretty sure I know all I need to know. Besides, I've lost my appetite." Then she left, letting the screen door bang shut behind her.

Dot sighed and looked apologetically at Jack.

"Was it something I said?" he asked.

Chapter eight

"He thinks he knows everything and that he's oh so irresistible, but worse than that, he thinks he's better than everyone around here," Maggie fumed, as she nursed a cold coke and dangled her legs off a tall bar stool.

Her friend Harper was behind the bar, pretending to wipe the counter top for her bosses benefit, but really just consoling her friend.

"He sounds like a giant pain in the ass," she observed. "I hate men who think they know everything."

"What I don't understand is why he keeps hanging around? I've made it perfectly clear I can't stand him."

"Perhaps he's one of those men who get off on the thrill of being rejected?"

"Maybe. He seems slightly smarter than that though."

"Perhaps he thinks he can win you over then, are you sure you made it crystal clear?"

"I told him I wouldn't date him even if he was the last man left alive on earth."

"Right. But did you say it like you really meant it?"

"Of course I did."

"Well then honey, I don't know what his problem is," Harper declared. A man came up to the bar for a refill and she quickly served him then turned her attention back to Maggie.

"So is he just passing through do you think?"

Maggie sighed, cupping her chin in her hands and resting her elbows on the bar.

"Who knows," she said. "I hope so."

"Is he good looking?"

"What's that got to do with anything?"

"I'm just curious."

Maggie pictured Jack. She was reluctant to admit it to her friend, but he was good looking, although not in the conventional way. There was something about the dimensions in his face that weren't quite right, but it worked for him.

"I guess so," she admitted reluctantly. "If you're attracted to that sort of guy."

"And what sort of guy is that?"

"Blond, tall, blue eyed. But don't forget arrogant, self assured and supremely confident."

Harper stopped wiping and frowned, "Wait, what did you say his name is again?"

"Jack Cartwright."

Harper turned to where her boss Wade, owner and operator of the bar and who also happened to be her boyfriend, was stocking one of the fridges.

"Wade baby, where have I heard the name Jack Cartwright before?"

Wade put the last beer inside and closed the door then he got up and dusted off his knees. "I think that bit of the counter is clean enough sweetheart," he teased, letting Harper know he was on to her. She flicked out at him with her cloth and laughing he grabbed her, holding her hands down at her sides and kissing her.

"Get a room you two," someone hollered.

"Ahem," Maggie coughed after a minute, when it seemed like they had forgotten to surface for air. They pulled apart and Harper pretended to straighten her hair.

"That," she pouted at Wade, "is workplace sexual harassment, and I would like to remind you that I could have you arrested for that."

"Be my guest, I've always wanted you to lock me up in handcuffs," he grinned.

Maggie groaned. "You two are so sickeningly in love," she complained. "

"Sorry," Harper said to her friend, and she did feel a little bit bad. Ever since Jon had left, leaving Maggie high and dry with a young Willow and no income to support herself, she had been itching for her friend to find someone new and have the same kind of happiness she had. But Maggie had never shown any interest in anyone of the opposite sex, focusing only on Willow and building her business.

"It's ok," Maggie said. "It gives me hope that not all men are no hopers like Jon, or conceited know-it-all's like Jack."

"Oh right," Harper remembered her earlier question. "Baby, do we know a Jack Cartwright?"

"Know him? No. Know *of* him, yes."

"Sounds ominous."

"Not at all. From what I hear, he's made quite the impression already."

"On who?"

"Locals," Wade said, "both the two-legged and the four-legged variety."

Maggie frowned. "What are you on about?"

"He's the new Veterinarian in town. Moved here to replace old Bob Hawkins who's retiring."

"Oh no," Maggie covered her eyes with her hands and started moaning.

"What's wrong?" Harper asked in alarm.

"That means he's not just passing through," Maggie wailed, "he's here for good."

"He's really got under your skin hasn't he," Wade observed. "Sounds to me like someone maybe has piqued your interest a little?"

"Don't talk crazy," Maggie said. "I've already said I can't stand the guy."

"Methinks the lady doth protest too much," said Harper.

"Well methinks the bar lady should keep her opinions to herself and pour the customer another drink. Something stronger this time."

"Wine?"

"Stronger."

"Coming right up ma'am," Harper saluted, grabbing a glass from below the counter and the whiskey bottle off the shelf behind her. She poured one shot into it.

"Don't be stingy," Maggie said, "and don't call me ma'am."

"You're not normally a big day drinker," observed Wade.

"Yeah, well nothing about the last two days seems normal, so there."

Sometime later, after plenty of chatter and laughing and three games of darts with some of the other patrons, all of which she lost, she checked her watch and realised that she'd better be getting home. The sun had started to sink lower in the sky which meant Willow would be making her way home, fish or no fish. She would stay out all night if she could; "the fish always bite better in the dark," she'd protested once before when Maggie had been forced to go and fetch her back home.

"Thanks for listening," she said to Harper, stepping up onto the foot rest that ran around the bar and leaning over the bar to kiss her friend on the cheek, to catcalls and whistles from some of the local men.

"Anytime my sweet, you know where I am. Give that gorgeous little girl of yours a big kiss from Aunty Harper."

"I'll try. Sadly she's not big on the soppy stuff anymore."

Maggie drove home in a much better mood than when she had left. She wound down the window, enjoying the intoxicating mix of smells the world offered at sunset. They swirled throughout her car and tugged at her hair. She felt refreshed and invigorated, as a few hours with a best friend can do for you.

Pulling into her driveway and getting out of the car, she hesitated; she was reluctant to leave the beauty of the outside world for the confinement of wooden walls and electric lighting. So she wandered over to the big Magnolia tree beside the wire fence that framed the driveway. Next to it stretched acres and acres of empty paddocks, the couple nearest belonging to them but the ones after that belonging to the farmer next door. A ridge in the distance broke the endless fields, and although the sun had sunk behind it, it had only just gone, and its colours were still smeared across the sky like a messy child's painting.

Standing near the fence she stretched, like a cat after a nap, arching her back and extending her arms above her head to the sky. She sucked the fresh air deep inside her body and then exhaled in one long breath.

Life, she thought, doesn't get any more beautiful than this. There was nothing like a sunset to remind you look up and marvel at the great big world around you. Stars were starting to twinkle in the dusky sky.

Reluctantly accepting that she couldn't stay out here forever, she turned to go inside the house but then she saw the tyre swing her father had hung from the tree a long time ago, when she was about Willow's age. The ropes had been worn into the branch from relentless swinging, and the tyre itself had been replaced at least twice after the rubber, exposed to the elements, had become flimsy and cracked. She felt a childish urge come over her and succumbing to it, she climbed onto the swing, wrapping her arms around the ropes and her legs around the tire. Pushing off the ground over and over until she had a good swing going, she leant back and closed her eyes, enjoying the feel of the wind in her hair; whistling softly past her ears.

She was just starting to wind slowly to a stop when she felt strong hands on her back, pushing her gently off again. She smiled.

"Thanks," she said, thinking it was her father and wondering how many times his hands had pushed her on this same swing over the years.

"You're welcome."

Her eyes flew open and she tried to stop the swing, overbalancing and falling off so she landed on her backside in the grass.

"You ok?" Jack reached out a hand to help pull her up.

Ignoring it, she got up and wiped grass off her jeans. "What the hell is wrong with you, sneaking up on me like that?"

"I'm sorry, I thought you would have heard me. You were lost in your own little world though, I think."

"What are you still doing here?" she demanded, "you should be long gone by now." She looked past him. "And where is your car? Did you hide it or something?" Her tone was accusatory.

"Yes," he said. "That's exactly what I did. I hid my car behind a hedge so that I could lull you into a false sense of security, thinking that I was gone, but then BAM!" He smacked one fist into the other hand. "When you walked through the front door, there I would be, sitting at the dining table as plain as day and, according to you, up to no good."

"Ha ha, funny guy. That still doesn't explain where your car is."

"It's in the shed. Your father's bike wouldn't start so I had to jump start it."

"Oh great, what have you done to his bike?"

"I didn't do anything, it was like that when I got here, I swear."

"You must have done something."

"I hardly touched the thing. I don't have the first clue about the inner workings of anything mechanical."

"No, only animals from what I hear."

A smile spread across his face. "Why Maggie Tanner, have you been doing a little asking around town about me? I'm flattered."

She flushed, grateful it was dark enough for him not to notice.

"Don't be," she said. "I was devastated when I found out you're here for good."

"Ouch." He put a hand over his heart and shook his head sadly. Then his expression turned serious. "You really don't like me do you?" he asked.

Maggie shrugged and headed past him towards the house. "So far you haven't given me a whole lot to like."

"I know we got off on the wrong foot but I've apologized for that, more than once. I don't know what else I've done to upset you but I'd love to know so I can try and fix it."

Maggie paused, turning to him. "Why?" she asked. "Why do you care so much what I think about you?"

She was unnerved with the look he gave her when she asked this. All traces of his trademark humour and cheekiness were gone from his face. Without this armour he looked, *vulnerable*. She wasn't sure whether to trust it or whether it was just another trick he'd pulled from his arsenal.

"Well?" she asked.

"I like you," he said. When he saw her expression he hastily added, "Not like that. Just, you know, as a potential friend. Possibly. One day."

She regarded him sceptically.

"I haven't met many people since I've moved here that interest me in the way you and your family do," he carried on. "I find your parents charming and as for your daughter, well. Let's just say she's brightened up both of the days I've seen her."

"If you're having a go at my daughter again -"

"I'm not. I promise. She's a complete delight."

Maggie scanned his face. He features appeared genuine, but there was something else there also, something written across his face that made him seem a little lost. She decided to give him the benefit of the doubt.

"Thank you," she said. "As you've probably realised, Willow is everything to me. I'm sorry if I've been a little prickly.

I've been known to be slightly, *overprotective,* when it comes to my daughter."

A small smile tugged at his lips but disappeared again before she could be sure.

"Did you just smirk?" she asked.

"Of course not, it must have been a trick of the light."

"I sincerely hope so."

He stepped closer until he was within a step of her again, as he had been earlier in the day. The smell of him did something crazy to her breathing, making it shallow and raspy. She held it so he wouldn't hear, but she refused to take a step backwards.

"I promise you Maggie," he said in a low voice, "you have nothing to worry about. My intentions are pure."

"That's good to hear."

'Truce?"

"Alright, truce."

"Did anyone ever tell you that moonlight suits you," he whispered.

The intensity of the moment had almost robbed her of her voice but she managed to rescue a tiny spark.

"Why," she replied, "because it hides all my flaws?"

He chuckled, and then reached up a hand to softly brush a tendril of hair away from her face.

"No. Because it makes your skin and your eyes illuminated as if lit by a blue flame from within." he said. "And your lips shine as if crafted from the finest silver."

"Ahem," a voice coughed behind them and broke the spell. They both turned to see the silhouette of Dot standing in the open door. Maggie hurriedly took a step back from Jack.

"Hi mum," she said. "Is Willow home?"

"She's here," Dot answered. "Showered and tired but full to the brim with stories of how she landed her monster fish."

"I can't wait to hear them," Maggie's voice came out high pitched. She coughed to clear her throat.

"So are you two are planning on coming inside tonight?"

Maggie ignored this and pushed past her mother to get inside the house. Jack followed. The heat that emanated from them left scorch marks on the door frame as they passed, and a tiny spark leapt from Jack and singed Dot's hair.

"Ouch," she said, rubbing the spot. Her eyes followed them as they headed into the kitchen.

"Oh yes," she nodded to herself. "It's definitely obvious what's going to happen there."

Chapter nine

"What was that noise?" Ray looked around, confused. "Did someone let a cat in?"

"It was his stomach," Willow pointed at Jack with a fork.

"Don't point with your cutlery," said Maggie. "It's rude."

'Sorry," Jack looked sheepish. "It's just that it's been awhile since I've sat down to a meal so spectacular." He scanned the table eagerly, not sure where to start and keen to dive in but holding back out of politeness.

Dot had been busy in the kitchen for most of the afternoon. The lamb had been slow roasting for the past four hours, with sprigs of fresh picked rosemary from the bush underneath the kitchen window, and cloves of garlic poked deep into the flesh of the meat. It was brown and crispy on the outside, and as Ray carved it Jack could see that it was succulent and juicy on the inside. In the last hour at various times she'd added potatoes, carrots, yams, onions and parsnips to the pan, turning them occasionally and basting them with the fat from the lamb. The potatoes were the main thing catching Jack's eye and causing his stomach to growl hungrily. They looked crunchy and he just knew that when he bit into them the insides would be fluffy and perfect.

On a long platter in the middle lay the fish that Willow had caught that afternoon. It had been smoked until the flesh had turned golden. Now, the skin had been peeled back to reveal the delicate and juicy white meat.

There was also a bowl of baby peas, some corn on the cob, a plate with some fresh bread buns piled high and a blue pottery jug filled to almost overflowing with homemade gravy. Dot had also picked some bluebells that grew wild along the back fence and put them in a pretty crystal vase with some water. Their sweet, delicate scent spoke of summer days.

Jack's stomach growled again, and this time everyone heard it.

"Christ," said Ray, "you'd better hurry up and feed that man, Dot. Sounds like a famished bear that hasn't eaten all winter."

Dot surveyed the table, making sure she had everything. "Salt and Pepper." She fetched the tall grinders from the pantry, placing them in the centre of the table. "Right that's it, dig in."

Jack didn't need to be told twice. He grabbed tongs and serving spoons and he ladled and grabbed until there was no inch of his plate that wasn't covered in food. Only then did he sit back, ready to eat, and noticed the others all watching him in fascination.

"What?" he asked.

"Nothing," Dot snapped out of it and frowned at the others. "Stop staring at our guest," she said. "It's wonderfully refrshing to see a man with such a healthy appetite."

For awhile there was no noise but the sound of jaws chewing, but after a few minutes Willow remembered she hadn't told her mum the story of how she'd caught the fish and she started to relay it with gusto, hands gestures included.

"Don't talk with your mouth full," said Ray with his mouth full.

Willow rolled her eyes, but swallowed exaggeratedly and carried on with the story. Maggie listened indulgently, her eyes following the animation on her daughters face. She felt a surge of love for her daughter. Ever since she had been a newborn baby in her arms Maggie had considered Willow to be her finest achievement in life. It was the simplest moments like these, with her daughter and her family around her, that reminded her just how wonderful life could be. It didn't matter if they weren't rich. They had each other, and they had love.

She didn't realise that the love she was feeling inside was clearly visible on the outside, in the intensity of her eyes, the flush on her skin and the way she bit one corner of her lip lightly until it turned the colour of ripe plums.

Jack watched, captivated, and failed to hear when Ray asked him a question. Dot and Ray could see why and exchanged smug smiles. Willow noticed.

"What?" she said. "What are you guys smiling about?"

"Nothing, eat your peas."

"No, I don't like them."

"Since when?"

"Since you guys started getting all secretive. If you want me to eat my vegetables then tell me what's so secret all of a sudden."

Maggie sighed. "No one is keeping any secrets from you, baby," she said, hating the lie even as she spoke it. Dot's eyebrows shot up but she kept quiet. It wasn't her place. The air around the table had suddenly become thick and grey with tension.

Jack was puzzled. He knew he had missed something but whatever it was had gone right over his head. He pushed his now empty plate away and sat back, groaning theatrically.

"That was some feast," he said. "That should carry me through for a few days at least. Thank you," he smiled at Dot. "I can't remember the last time I enjoyed a meal more."

"You're very welcome," she said.

"You should be thanking *me* for the fish," pointed out Willow.

"Of course. Thank you, Willow, for catching such a monstrously delicious fish."

"You're welcome," she said. Then she added grudgingly, "Thank you for helping us smoke it."

"And who should I be thanking for the impressive piece of lamb? You, Ray?"

The silence that followed this innocuous question was immediate and hollow. He glanced from face to face. Maggie's eyes seemed to be shooting a message or warning of some sort his way, but without knowing what he had done he was powerless to prevent himself from doing it again. He frowned at her, trying to convey that he was clueless as to what he'd done wrong. The only one who seemed unperturbed was Willow.

"My dad gave it to us," she answered him, mopping up the last of the gravy off her plate with a bread roll, unaware of the volley of loaded stares that were shooting around the table over her head.

Ah, Jack thought. I've wandered into some kind of sensitive territory here. He knew from asking around town that Maggie's husband Jon had left her a few years back. No one seemed to know why or where he had gone, but that part was of little interest to Jack anyway. The only thing he'd cared about was that she was single. So when she had lied to him at the market and said she was married he was thrown, but figured it was simply a ploy to get him to leave her alone. Now though, he knew there was something more going on here.

"Does he live around these parts?" he asked casually.

"Yep. Well, sort of," Willow answered.

Maggie and Dot both leapt up from the table, gathering plates and bowls and clanging them together noisily in an effort to put an end to any more conversation. Maggie came around the table and on the pretence of leaning over him to grab his plate she took the opportunity to hiss in Jack's ear.

"Shut up," she said.

Jack pretended he hadn't heard.

"Do you see him often?" he directed this question at Willow.

"Nope."

"So only on holidays and special occasions?"

"Nope."

"Wait, surely you must see him sometimes?"

"No, never," she confirmed. She seemed unaffected by this startling declaration.

Maggie leant over Jacks shoulder again, this time elbowing him in his side sharply as she hissed louder. "*I told you to shut up.*"

Jack ducked out of reach of her elbow. "What do you mean, *never?*"

Willow finally looked up at him. "I mean never. And if you don't know the meaning of the word, look it up in a dictionary or go back to school. What's with all the questions anyway?"

"Sorry I'm just a little confused. I thought you said he gave you this meat."

"Yeah he did, and?"

Jack looked at the other adults. "Am I missing something?"

"Can I take the fatty scraps out to Rufus?" Willow asked.

'Sure honey," Dot scraped them all on to one plate and passed it to her. Maggie waited till she was out the door before she turned on Jack.

"Our family affairs are *none* of your business," she told him fiercely. She looked at the clock hanging on the wall over the sink. It was barely eight o'clock but she wanted him gone. Now.

"It's late," she said. "I'm sure you need to get going."

"But there's still dessert –" Dot protested. She had made a blackberry and apple crumble and fresh custard.

"Hmm, that sounds –"

"I think Jack has had enough to eat for one night, mother. We don't want to make him ill from dining on too much good food do we?" Her tone implied that she wished him very ill indeed.

"There's always room for –"

"I'm sure Jack mentioned he has an early start tomorrow. And I need to make sure Willow's things are ready for school."

"But —"

Maggie yawned, exaggeratedly. "I'll see you out," she glared at Jack.

He registered the angry glint in her eye and decided he'd better not push things any further. This town was home for the foreseeable future, and there would be plenty of time later to unravel the mystery. He pushed back his chair.

"Lift it, don't scrape it," said Ray.

"Thank you," Jack said to Dot, "for such a wonderful day. I've enjoyed both meals immensely, and I hope I haven't overstayed my welcome so much that I won't be invited back again."

"Don't bet on it," Maggie muttered.

Dot embraced Jack. "Don't be silly. "We've loved having you around, haven't we Ray?"

"Sure."

"I'll see if I can find anything out about your model of bike," Jack said. "Do a little research on the computer."

"Or he could just do what normal people do and take it to a mechanic," Willow came back inside with a plate that looked suspiciously like it had been licked clean.

"And pay through the nose for them to spend hours fixing it when I'm perfectly capable of doing it myself? Not likely."

Dot sighed. "You aren't capable, that's the whole point."

"Blasphemy. You shouldn't insult a man's skills like that."

Dot rolled her eyes. "Whatever."

Jack smiled; he was starting to see a pattern here. Then he saw Maggie's face and stopped smiling.

"Er, right," he said. "I'd best get going. Early start and all that. Night all."

"I'll come out and lock up the shed after you," Maggie said.

Once they had left the room Ray winked at Dot, who nodded.

"What's up with that?" asked Willow.

"What's up with what?"

"The secret signals you guys keep giving each other."

Ray reached over and ruffled Willow's hair.

"Don't know what you're talking about kid."

"Get off," she said, pushing her chair back.

"Lift it, don't scrape it."

"You guys think you're so clever but you wait, I'll find out what's going on," muttered Willow, heading off to her bedroom.

Outside, Maggie waited until they were almost at the shed before she rounded on Jack, jabbing at his chest with a finger.

"Just what the hell do you think you're playing at," she demanded furiously.

"Whoa," he took a step back and held up his hands defensively. "I thought we'd declared a truce." He whistled for Rufus who came bounding from the warm spot he'd been occupying on the front porch.

"That was before you started sticking your nose in where it doesn't belong."

"I was just being polite."

"No, you were being nosy."

"Alright, so what if I was?"

"Aha, you admit it then."

"Well how else am I supposed to find out anything about you? You're not exactly forthcoming with any details."

"But that's just it; you don't *need* to know anything about me. We're not friends, and with the ay you're carrying on we're unlikely ever to be."

They reached the garage and she felt for the light switch on the wall, flicking it down into the on position.

"You really don't hold anything back, do you?" he mused. "You just say whatever's on your mind."

"No and I don't see why I should. Honesty up front is the only way to be. It's the only way to be sure no one will end up getting hurt."

As she said the last part he saw her eyes darken, and she sighed ever so softly. She seemed to have left him momentarily, her mind searching back in on itself, reliving some memory.

"Who hurt you?" he asked gently, his fingers itchy at his side with the longing to reach out and comfort her. It took all his willpower to stop them.

She snapped back into focus and shook her head, banishing whatever memory it was that had assailed her. "I don't know what you're talking about." She folded her arms in front of her body defensively to create a barrier between them.

"I really need to go and help Willow get ready for school tomorrow," she said.

"Of course," he smiled in an effort to lighten the mood. If there was one thing he was learning, it was that Maggie would not be pushed. He would have to be patient, something that was unfortunately not his strong suit.

He got into his car and started the engine then he wound down the window. "Maybe we could meet up sometime this week? Grab a coffee or a bite to eat?"

She shook her head again. "I don't think so. I'm pretty busy at the moment, with the lead up to Christmas and everything that comes with it."

"I understand," he said. "But if you change your mind or get some free time, call me. I left my number with your mother."

She murmured noncommittally, wanting him to leave.

He left, driving slowly off down the driveway, his eyes in the rear view mirror watching as she closed the garage doors and headed back towards the house.

She intrigued him; to the point where he had spent hours last night lying awake in his bed, watching the crack around the curtain become lighter and lighter, thinking about her. He would just have to bide his time

Chapter ten

"You're being paranoid."

"I am not. There's something going on that they're not telling me, I'm sure of it."

"Like what?"

"That I don't know. But I'm going to find out."

Willow lay on her side next to the creek and dangled her fingers in the cool water. The sun was warm on her back, and she knew it wouldn't be long before they would be swimming in the creek every chance they could get, but for now the water was still a touch icy from the water coming down off the hills.

Nick sat beside her with his fishing hand line dangling down into the water. Beside him a small blue plastic bucket writhed with the worms they had dug up on the way to the creek after school. The second the three o'clock bell had chimed they'd been out the door before the teacher had even finished speaking. They walked the long way to the creek which took them through a part of town where pretty little gardens bordered by tidy little hedges were well maintained by proud elderly. They'd discovered the best worms in town came from these gardens; fat and complacent from dining on the finest compost. The trick was digging out the worms without anyone noticing, and usually one would kick at the dirt while the other kept watch for twitching curtains that signalled they'd been spotted by someone inside.

Every now and then a trout would break the surface causing ripples, but so far they were resisting his bait, despite the particularly fat worm he had on the end of his line at the moment.

"All I know," Willow continued, "is that it started around the time Jack came on the scene."

"You think it has something to do with him?"

"Duh that's what I just said."

"Duh yourself. Do you like him? What's he like?"

Willow shrugged her shoulders. "He's ok I guess. He helped granddad and I smoke the fish yesterday, stripped some bark off the Manuka tree to put in which gave it a nice flavour."

"You think he and your mum might –?"

She waited for him to finish the sentence but he didn't. She rolled over and looked up at him quizzically. "Might what?"

"You know, start dating."

"Eww, no way. Mum's not interested in dating, she told me. Anyway, even if she was it wouldn't be with him. She can't stand him."

Nick didn't say anything, but she could tell from the way he raised his eyebrows that he had something to say that he was holding back.

"What?" she asked.

"Nothing."

"Bullshit nothing. I can tell you got something on your mind so spit it out."

"You promise you won't hit me?"

"How can I promise when I don't know what you're going to say? You might say something that makes me *want* to hit you."

"Then I'm not saying nothing."

"You can't not say it now," she said stroppily, "you got me all curious."

"Promise."

"Fine," she snapped. "I promise." But she crossed her fingers behind her back as she said it.

"Say it again without crossing your fingers."

Her mouth fell open. "How did you -?"

"Willow, I've known you since you were six years old. I know when you're bullshitting me."

She flounced back down on to her back and closed her eyes.

"I don't care anymore anyway," she said.

"Yes you do."

"Fine. I do. So just say it already."

"Your mum is still only young, as far as old people go. And," he shuffled away from Willow on the grass, "she's really, *really,* pretty."

Willow lashed out at him.

"Don't you *dare* talk about my mum like that!"

"I'm only saying what all the boys say. Out of all the mum's at school, yours is by far the prettiest and the only one any of us would consider kissing."

"You guys are disgusting. I can't believe you talk about my mum like that!"

Nick shrugged. "We're boys," he said. "It's what we do."

"Well boys are idiots."

"No one's arguing with you there."

Willow stewed silently. The only sounds were birds chirping in the trees and a gentle breeze causing leaves on the weeping willow above the bank to rustle.

"What's that got to do with anything anyway?" Willow finally asked.

"I just think you need to open your eyes is all. Your mum can't stay single forever, she deserves a little happiness." He didn't mention that he was quoting this last bit directly from something he'd heard his mother say to his father not long ago.

"I've never stopped her from seeing anyone."

"Well, you have kind of. But not on purpose"

"I have not."

Nick pulled his line out of the water and sighed when he saw the hook was empty. He fished around in the bucket for the next fattest worm. "Have you asked her what's up with your dad lately?"

Willow rolled back towards him and cupped her face in her hands, resting on her elbows. "You know I haven't. You think that's why she doesn't date anyone? She's waiting for him to come back?"

"No I don't think that's it. But maybe she thinks *you* are waiting for him to come back."

Willow frowned at him. "I stopped waiting for that to happen years ago."

"But have you told your mum that?"

"Of course not. She's still keeping up this ridiculous pretence with the meat each Sunday."

"Yeah, that has kind of gone on for a bit long now."

"Exactly. At first I knew she was doing it to make me feel better, so I went along with it. And now I can't exactly admit that I know what she's been up to all these years, can I?"

Nick drew an arm back and threw the hook and worm out into the water. It landed with a plop then sank slowly.

"I guess not," he said.

Willow sighed and reached out to pick a handful of daisies. She started piercing holes in the stems with a fingernail and threading them through each other to make a daisy chain.

"I don't know," she said. "It's all too bloody complicated."

Chapter eleven

A week and later Maggie could no longer ignore it.

It started when she drove through Main Street on the way to the supermarket and saw council workers hanging strings of coloured fairy lights in the big Angel Oak, on top of the ones that were still hanging in there from the night of the market.

"Surely not," she said to herself.

Then at the supermarket, near the checkouts, she saw displays of chocolate advent calendars, marked down to clear.

"It's a bit early isn't it?" she muttered. "And why are they reduced?"

Then, back at home, as she was unpacking the groceries in the kitchen she turned on the stereo for a bit of background noise and the unmistakable opening notes of men singing stopped her in her tracks.

"No, it can't be," she said, her face ashen.

But it was.

"Turn it up!" said Dot. "'I love this song." Then she danced around the lounge room singing along to Snoopy's Christmas. "*Christmas bells, those Christmas bells, ringing through the land –*"

Maggie watched her mother twirling for a minute, and then she crossed to the fridge and studied the calendar.

"No," she squeezed her eyes shut and opened them again but the fact remained the same. There were only just under three weeks left till Christmas.

"Where did the time go? How can it be upon us again already? So soon?" she asked no one in particular, as she sank into a kitchen chair and dropped her head into her hands. The song finished and her mother turned the stereo down and wandered into the kitchen. She flicked the switch down to boil the jug.

"Don't be so dramatic," she told her daughter. "This is the most joyous time of the year."

"Yes I'm aware you feel that way mother. You say the same thing every year."

"And every year you grumble and groan and act like the Grinch who got nothing but a potato in his stocking."

"I do not."

"You do too."

"Whatever."

Dot put two teabags in mugs and poured hot water over them. While they soaked she regarded her daughter, who had started flicking through one of the many brochures advertising potential gifts that got stuffed into their mailbox this time of year.

"Look at all this rubbish," Maggie said cynically. "Designed to drive people broke trying to outdo each other to see who can buy the best present."

"Says you, who counts on the Christmas sales of your soaps," Dot says with eyebrows raised.

"That's different and you know it. I don't push my products on anyone, they seek me out. My soaps actually help people, not like this plastic crap," she pushed some of the brochures lying on the table in front of her, "that breaks down three days after Christmas. And my prices aren't so bad you need to take out a second mortgage come January."

"*Some* people and companies see Christmas as a commercial cash cow, yes," Dot admitted. "But it doesn't have to be all about money, you know that. Don't you remember the Christmases I gave you when you were young? The magic you sensed, the wonder you felt?"

Maggie sighed. "Yes, of course I remember. It's just hard to sustain the magic when you're an adult trying to pay the bills."

Ah, Dot thought. She knew where this was coming from now. Ever since Jon had left Maggie had done her absolute hardest to fulfil the roles of both parents. She felt guilty that her child had become the product of a single parent home, mostly because she blamed herself for his departure, and she was determined that Willow would never feel different to any other

119

child in her class. And that meant she would have exactly the same as they had.

"She doesn't need lots of things, you know that," Dot said gently, placing Maggie's tea down in front of her and fetching a packet of Gingernuts from the cupboard to dunk. "She has love, she has a roof over her head and she has food in her belly. She has fresh air and a vivid imagination that helps her see the world as her playground. It's all she needs."

"I know mum," Maggie said. "But I still wish I could buy her everything she deserves."

"But she doesn't want for anything. Even if you were able to buy her all the best toys in the world, you know they'd sit neglected and dusty in her room, while she and Nick were out climbing trees and swimming in the creek."

"I know, you're right," Maggie sighed.

"You've raised a wonderful girl. She is clever and has her head screwed on straight. Stop being so hard on yourself."

"Thanks mum." Maggie reached over and gave her mother's hand an affectionate squeeze.

"You're welcome. Oh bugger," she peered into her mug, "I held my biscuit in for too long and now it's dropped off." She went to the drawer to fetch a teaspoon to fish the offending biscuit out. Something out the window caught her eye.

"Oh what's he up to now?" she asked. She could see Ray had wheeled the bike out of the shed and was connecting it

120

with wires to a battery pack sitting on the ground. She pushed opened the window above the sink.

"What are you doing to that thing now?" she called.

Ray looked up. "Mind your own business."

"Fine, but don't go calling me when you end up in a ditch, you crazy old bastard!" She slammed the window shut.

"I swear that man could try the patience of a saint," she grumbled to Maggie.

"Yet somehow you've put up with him for nearly fifty years" Maggie said.

"Yes, and I deserve more than a medal let me tell you."

"How do you guys do it? How have you stayed together through all the drama life has thrown at you over the years?"

Dot was surprised by the question but she didn't let it show on her face. Maggie wasn't one for deep conversations, not with her family at least. In fact, Dot was so used to her daughter keeping her feelings and emotions close to her chest that it took her a minute or two to rally an answer.

"I don't honestly know," she admitted. "I guess back in my day, when you stood in front of that altar and you promised yourself to each other, you just knew it was for the rest of your life. There was never any question of otherwise. You pledged your love in thick and thin, blah, blah, blah, and you stuck to it. No matter how hard it got, or how many times you could easily have killed him over the years. And believe me, there were plenty of those."

"You were never tempted to throw in the towel?"

"Oh I was tempted plenty of times. There were days I packed a suitcase for you and I and we got as far as the end of the driveway. But I always came back."

"Why?"

Dot looked towards the window where Ray was bent over the bike.

"I love the crazy old fool," she said simply. "He drives me insane and there are times I can't stand the sight of him, but I do love him."

"And that's enough?"

"It is."

Maggie sighed heavily.

"What's on your mind love?" her mother asked, concerned. "Is everything ok?"

"Oh nothing, nothing at all. I'm fine."

"Is it because of Jack? Has he got you thinking this way?"

"Of course not. Don't talk crazy." Maggie sat back up straight again and scowled at her mother. "I don't know why you would even mention him."

"Sorry love," her mother soothed, but secretly she was thinking that she'd struck a nerve.

Maggie checked her watch, "I better go," she said. "I want to get some Christmas wrapping paper before the shop shuts. People will be asking me to gift wrap their purchases soon."

She scowled again as she headed for the door.

"Do try and capture some Christmas spirit," her mother called after her. "For Willow's sake at least."

She watched her daughter leave, then went and poured some more hot water over her tea bag. She knew this time of year was always a little hard on Maggie, but this year she seemed to be taking it particularly hard.

Jon had left at Christmas; two days before the big day to be precise. He had just upped and gone into the night after an argument according to Maggie, and no one had seen him nor heard from him since. Dot knew that Maggie blamed herself to a degree. From the little she'd told her parents, things hadn't been quite right between them for some time. They'd been arguing a lot, mostly about Jon's footloose and fancy free ways. He thought nothing of taking off hunting with friends for weeks at a time, emerging from the mountains filthy and hairy and triumphantly showing off whatever he'd killed as if he expected Maggie to be grateful.

Dot shook off her melancholy. She had wasted enough time thinking of the man who had hurt her daughter. She breathed in deep and then let it out in one long exhale. The air that exited her lungs was tinged blue with disappointment, grey with regret and with red flecks of anger. Heaving with the dark emotions it sank slowly to the floorboards. Dot picked up a broom from the corner and swept it out the back door.

"Be gone with you," she said, as she closed the door on it. "This is a joyous time of year and I will not let that man ruin another Christmas for this family." She went to the cupboard and pulled out the ingredients to bake another Christmas cake, even though she had already prepared two. Soon, the house would be filled with the merry smells of fruit and liquor and almond icing. That would perk Maggie up for sure.

Driving into town, Maggie blinked back tears as she also reflected on the past. Damn that man for tainting this time of the year for her. She could remember a time when she loved Christmas, when it was her favourite time of the year. But *he'd* ruined that for her. When Jon had shown up that last time having been AWOL for ten days, flourishing a wild pig at her and grinning like a Cheshire cat, she hadn't been grateful to see him at all. She'd been furious.

"Where the hell have you been?" she'd demanded of him.

"Whoa," he'd said, taking a step back. "What's wrong with you?"

"What's wrong with me? Jon, you buggered off again with no warning, no explanation, not even a note. I have no idea if you're dead or alive or when you'll be back. You promised to stop this kind of behaviour when Willow was born."

"No, you *asked* me to promise. I did no such thing and I don't see what the problem is."

"Are you serious? Jon, you're a father now. We have a beautiful little girl who depends on you, or have you forgotten that? You can't keep living like you're eighteen and only pleasing yourself, it's not fair on her or me."

"Man you never used to be like this," he'd said.

'Like what?"

"Like this. You're such a bitch these days. Remember when we first got together and we promised each other that we wouldn't bow to society's rules; that we'd do whatever we wanted whenever we wanted and screw everyone else."

She'd sighed and rubbed her temples warily. "Yes Jon, I remember. I also remember we were pretty drunk at the time. But we grew up, or at least I did. We have a child now. You have to start thinking of her. I had to sell some of our belongings just to make the rent this month. I can't live like this, unpredictably, worrying about where the next pay check is going to come from. You haven't held down a job for longer than six months and I'm already working two. It's not fair." She started to cry.

"Oh here we go again with the waterworks," he'd snarled. "You do everything and I do nothing, blah, blah, blah. Same old fucken broken record."

"Well it's true," she'd cried. "What have you done lately to help this family out? Tell me, I can't *wait* to hear the answer. Your daughter is lying awake in bed with a rumbling tummy because I only had a packet of noodles to give her for her dinner. Do you know how that makes me feel?"

"What the hell do you think this is," he'd shouted, kicking the pig where it lay on the ground between them. Its head lolled to one side and its lifeless eyes seemed to stare at her. It made her even sadder.

"It's a pig Jon, I'm not blind."

'It's food for us for a month is what it is," he'd countered.

And she had known that it was pointless arguing. He really believed that disappearing into the bush for weeks at a time, leaving his wife and daughter to fend for themselves, with no money and no idea of when he would be back, was alright. As long as he bought back a pig or a goat or a deer, anything they could cook and eat, everything was ok.

So frustrated and tired of arguing, she'd waited till he was out of the shower and threw a pillow at him, telling him to sleep in the spare room that night. In the morning she woke with a fresh perspective, determined they would sort things out and that the marriage could be saved for Willow's sake. She would compromise, and she hoped he would too. But he was gone again. And as the days turned into weeks which turned into months, she finally realised this time his absence was for good, and he wasn't coming back.

So she'd given notice on her flat and moved back home with her parents; tail between her legs and licking her wounds, and she'd promised herself that Willow would never know that her father had chosen a life of freedom over a life with her. She'd sat her cherubic, chubby perfect little daughter down one day and told her that daddy had gone to live in the hills so that he could hunt lots of animals and bring them lots of meat so that they would never go hungry again. And every Sunday she got up in the very early hours of the morning and fetched whichever cut of meat she'd purchased earlier in the week and hidden in the shed freezer, and she put it in a chilly bin on the front porch with some ice packs to keep it cold overnight and she let her daughter believe that her father had left it there for them.

And Willow had never questioned it.

A loud horn behind her bought her back to the present day and to the realisation that the light in front of her had turned green.

"Sorry," she mouthed into her rear view mirror at the car behind. The lady waved back with a smile.

Maggie turned into a park and turned the car off.

"Damn you Jon Tanner," she said softly, "wherever you are. I hope it was worth it."

Chapter twelve

After purchasing some Christmas wrapping paper, colourful sparkly ribbons and a roll of sticky tape, Maggie threw them all into the backseat of her car, slammed the door shut and leant against it. She was twitchy and restless. Thinking about the past always did that to her. She checked her watch, 4.15pm. She didn't feel like heading home yet.

There was something about this time of year, the expectation that tickled the back of your neck, the feeling like at any moment a random passersby might burst into carol singing and snow might fall from the sky.

Damn holiday movies.

Even she, who found this time of year the hardest time of all, couldn't ignore the flickering you got deep down in your belly when you thought about Christmas.

She got in the car and without a conscious thought she headed to The Corner Pub. Harper was busy once again behind the bar. She smiled broadly when she saw her friend walk in.

"Twice in one week?" Harper said. "To what do I owe the pleasure?"

Maggie climbed onto a bar stool and sighed at her friend.

"Coke please. No wait, make it a cider."

"Which one?"

"The one with the highest percentage of alcohol."

Harpers pulled a face. "Day drinking? Again? Why do I get the feeling that something, or someone perhaps, is troubling you."

"It's nearly five. And don't you start," Maggie said. "I've already had Mum trying to get me to admit to something that hasn't and never will happen."

"Like what?"

"Nice try."

Harper decided to go easy on her friend. She knew this time of year was difficult for Maggie. She, Maggie and Jon had all gone to school together. In fact both girls had developed crushes on the ruggedly handsome first fifteen rugby player in their final year of high school, but it was Maggie who had caught Jon's eye. He'd been unreliable even back then but still Harper would never have picked he would desert Maggie and Willow like he had. If she knew where to find him she would kick his ass from here to Timbuktu, but it was like he had dropped off the face of the earth.

From time to time there had been unconfirmed sightings. Old school friends would say they had seen him in another town, from a distance, never close enough to speak too. Harper had even thought at one point about hiring a private detective to try and trace him, just so Maggie could get some closure. But Wade had talked her out of it.

"Don't interfere," he'd warned. "Let sleeping dogs lie. No good can come from raking up the past."

And as much as he and his idioms annoyed her, she knew he was right. But seeing her friend morose like this every Christmas was hard. She knew it wasn't because Maggie still loved Jon, those feelings had long since dissipated into the night, but it broke Maggie's heart that Jon never contacted Willow. Sweet, feisty little Willow.

"Here," Harper said, plonking a larger than normal glass down in front of her friend. "It's on the house."

After calling home and making sure that Willow was ok, Maggie insisted on paying for the next one, and the one after that.

"Maggie, you know you can't handle too much alcohol before you go all maudlin and silly" Harper gently reminded her friend.

"You're probably right," Maggie agreed. "But I don't care. It's Christmas. Aren't I supposed to drink and be merry at Christmas? Isn't that what you all want from me?"

"No sweet pea, we just want you to be happy."

"I *am* happy. I'm perfectly happy with my life thank you very much. It's you lot that seem to think I need something more."

"If you're talking about a man, I know you don't *need* one. I just think it would be nice for you to remember how much fun they can be."

"It all comes back to sex with you doesn't it."

"Well how long has it been exactly?"

"None of your business."

Harper whistled. "That long huh?"

"Shut up."

"You know what? I'm due a break. How about I join you."

"Oh that would be lovely," Maggie said gratefully.

While Harper finished up and told Wade and the other barman that she was finishing, Maggie nursed her drink and stewed. It *had* been a long time, longer than she would care to admit. Since Jon there had been only one other man and she preferred to forget all about him. It was a one off drunken fumble in the hay bales at a Guy Fawkes party a few years back with a farm hand from a few farms over. He was almost ten years younger than her for Christ's sakes, and she'd been deeply embarrassed when she woke the next morning and realised what they'd done. He on the other hand thought what they'd done was pretty damn awesome, and he'd been super keen on a repeat, something she'd made clear was never going to happen. Thankfully no one else had found out, and she planned on keeping it that way.

Here she was, in her prime, and as celibate as a nun. But it honestly hadn't bothered her until now. Why all of a sudden was she even thinking about this? She knew why, it was that damn Jack. He was pompous and rude, but hell, when he'd touched her she felt like someone had just jumpstarted her with an electric current. It had shot through her body, turning on switches, firing up cylinders and cranking handles. Now it was all she could think about.

"I need another drink," she drained the last of the pale liquid from her glass.

"Me too," agreed Harper, who upended her glass of wine and skulled the whole lot in one go. "Barkeep," she called, licking her lips, "two more drinks if you will. And make it quick."

"Only if you two eat something to line your stomachs," Wade said. "I don't need you vomiting on my damn floors. I'll get the chef to rustle you up a burger and fries each."

"Fine," they agreed to appease him, but when the food arrived they barely touched it. They were having too much fun drinking and reminiscing.

"Oh let's sing," said Harper, her eyes bright. "Baby chuck me the key to turn on the Karaoke machine," she called to Wade.

"Now now my darling," he said in a low voice, "you remember what you promised the last time?"

The Karaoke machine sat in the corner with a cloth draped over it, and was only used occasionally when the pub was hired out as a party venue. A year previously though Harper and a couple of other girlfriends had got plastered and decided to hold their own party, and some city guys passing through videoed them singing on their phone and uploaded it to You Tube. The clip had gone viral and gained over a hundred thousand views in one month. But not because it was any good. The women, who could barely stand they were so drunk, sounded like castrated cats scratching at metal bin lids. Harper had been mortified when she'd sobered up.

"Oh nah it's all good," she slurred, looking around the pub. "There's only locals here. None of them would dare video us, would you," she yelled.

"Baby I really think –"

"Pass me the bloody key or I'll get it myself," she growled.

He sighed and threw it over.

Soon she and Maggie were happily singing away to ABBA and a collection of songs from the movie Grease.

"Aw bugger it you two, you're scaring all my customers away," Wade complained as yet another couple paid hurriedly for their meal and left.

134

An hour later and Wade knew that neither woman would be capable of seeing themselves home. He went out the back to the kitchen and placed a call to Dot.

"I haven't seen her like this since Jon left," he told her quietly, one hand pushing the swinging door slightly open so he could keep an eye on the two.

Dot sighed. "I know. She was like that earlier today. Something is bothering her, more than normal I mean, for this time of year."

"You want me to bring her home?"

"No it's ok, I'll sort something. Just keep her there and keep her happy."

"Oh she's happy alright," he said wincing as the two of them murdered Bonnie Tyler's Total Eclipse of the Heart.

"What on earth is that racket?"

"Let's just say I think you better get here quick, before I have no business left."

It wasn't Dot or Ray though that walked through the door half an hour later, it was Jack. He scanned the room and spotted Maggie in the corner near the Karaoke machine. She had her head thrown back and microphone pressed against her lips as she gave a powerfully loud, if not tuneful, rendition of Sweet Caroline by Neil Diamond. Jack walked up to the bar and ordered a whiskey on the rocks.

The drink was placed in front of him and he took a large gulp. "Thanks," he smiled at Wade, "I have a feeling I'm going to need this." He watched the two women, amused, as they started singing Waterloo.

"Yeah sorry about them," Wade apologised, eyeing the two ladies who were oblivious to anything or anyone around them. "I was just about to shut the bar up. No point staying open when they're scaring all my customers away. I'm surprised you were brave enough to come through the door, could you not hear them from outside?"

"Oh yes I heard them alright. I heard them the moment I turned the corner onto the street." Jack shuddered as a particularly high note was attempted, and failed. "Can't you flick an off switch at the wall or something?"

Wade shrugged his shoulders. "Not much I can do about it sorry. The tall one is my girlfriend. She'd kill me if I pulled the plug."

"Ah I see," Jack smiled in understanding.

"Exactly. But while I may not have a choice in being here, you can still get out. Go; make a run for it while you still have your hearing."

"I would but I'm here on a mission."

Wade gave him a questioning look.

"I've been sent by Dot to collect the short one," Jack told him, gesturing towards the women.

"Maggie?"

"That's the one." He drained the rest of his whiskey, put his glass back on the counter then held out a hand, "Jack."

"Ah, understanding dawns," Wade shook Jack's hand. "I've heard about you."

"Christ, nothing too bad I hope."

"Well," Wade pulled a diplomatic face, "Let's just say that it can take Maggie a little time to warm up to new people."

"So I'm learning."

"Once she's your friend though she's as loyal as anything."

The song finished and Harper turned to holler at Wade.

"More drinks," she called.

"No," he said firmly. "You've had enough. It's time to go home now baby and get some water and aspirins into you."

"Boo spoilsport," she pouted. "I feel fine."

"Maybe you do right now," he said, "but I guarantee tomorrow morning you won't be feeling so crash hot." In an aside to Jack he added, "or looking it, if past experience is anything to go by."

Jack smirked and for the first time Maggie noticed him.

"*You*," she said.

"Yep, me," he answered cheerfully.

She turned to Harper. "It's him," she whispered loudly. "That Jack guy I told you about. I think he's stalking me."

"You should call the police," Harper whispered loudly back.

"That's a good idea."

Maggie turned to Wade and Jack. "Excuse me, but do either of you have a phone I could borrow? It's a local call."

"Now Maggie you're not going to go calling the police," Wade sighed.

"And why not?"

"Because you're talking all crazy. Honestly, who in their right mind would stalk you with all *your* baggage?"

"Hey, I resent that," Maggie protested.

"Well it's true. Get over yourself and give the guy a chance. I'm sure he has things he'd rather be doing than giving up his time to make sure you get home safely."

"I don't need a ride home."

"Yes, you do."

"Ok maybe I do. But not from him."

"Fine by me," Jack got up and headed towards the door.

"Good one Maggie," Wade said, "now what are you going to do, walk?"

"You can give me a ride home."

"No I can't. I have my hands full looking after this one," Wade said, trying to prop up Harper.

"Then I'll sleep here."

Wade sighed. "Just accept his offer of a ride and get out of my bar Maggie. And you know I say that with love."

Feeling more sober, Maggie turned towards the door that had just shut behind Jack. She kissed both Harper and Wade on the cheek then ran outside. Jack was in the driver's seat of his truck and just closing the door.

"Wait," she called.

He shut the door, turned the key in the ignition and wound down the window. "Yes?"

"Fine."

"Fine what?"

"Fine, you can take me home."

"Funny, I never heard the word please anywhere in that sentence."

She took a deep breath and counted to five before answering. "You want me to beg?"

"No, I want you to use your manners."

"What am I, five?"

"You tell me. You certainly act that age sometimes."

Outside the temperature had dropped, and Maggie was still dressed for the warm afternoon sun. Her bare shoulders shivered.

"*Please* can you take me home," she said through clenched teeth.

"That's better," he grinned. "Hop on in."

In the truck he turned the heater on low and the warm air from the vents made her feel drowsy. She rested her head against the headrest and closed her eyes, lulled by the gentle sound of the tyres turning on the road.

"Here," he said.

She opened her eyes, annoyed at the intrusion, and saw he was holding out an unopened bottle of water.

"No thanks."

"You'll feel better in the morning if you drink this now."

"I'm not drunk, if that's what you're implying."

"Would I dare?"

"For your information, I nursed the same drink for the last two hours. It's Harper you should be worried about. She'll be suffering tomorrow for sure."

"Still, you might be parched from all that, *singing*." He said it looking ahead with a straight face but still she thought she could hear the echo of laughter in his voice.

"Are you making fun of me?" she asked.

"Again, would I dare do that?"

Now that he had bought it up all she could feel was a scratching in the back of her throat. She coughed and when that didn't clear the itch she begrudgingly took the water.

"Thanks."

"Don't mention it."

"What were you doing at the bar this late anyway?" she asked after taking a long swig from the bottle. He was right; the water instantly revived her parched veins.

"Your mother called and asked me to make sure you got home ok."

Maggie was mortified. "She did?" She leant back in her seat again and shook her head.

"That interfering woman," she said grumpily.

"Come on, that's a bit harsh," Jack frowned. "She was worried about you. Said you're not normally a big drinker."

"What else did she say?"

He shrugged. "Nothing."

Her eyes narrowed. "I don't believe you. Spill."

"She might have mentioned that you struggle a little bit this time of year."

Maggie was furious. "Oh yeah? And did she happen to mention why?" If her mother had told Jack about Jon she would kill her.

"No she didn't," he took his eyes off the road for a second and looked at her. "I promise you that's all she said." But even though he sounded sincere she wasn't sure whether or not to believe him.

"How could she?" she asked, more to herself than him.

"She was just concerned for you. She is your mother after all, it's her job. Tell me you wouldn't be the same if it was Willow who needed help."

"I don't need your help. I most certainly didn't ask for it."

"So you would have been ok walking home in the dark this late by yourself?"

"I would have found my own way home, yes."

"You want me to let you out here?" he slowed the car down slightly. She glared at him, aware that he held all the cards at that moment.

"God you are so annoying," she said. "How could she even think I'd be interested in you?"

His eyebrows shot up.

"You're interested in me?"

"No!"

"But you just said -?"

"That's not what I said and you know it. I said *my mother* likes you."

"Your mother is interested in me?"

"Stop it!"

"Stop what?"

"Stop misreading my words on purpose."

"Sorry," he grinned again.

He turned onto the road that led out of town and towards her house. She studied him sideways out of the corner of her eye without him knowing. She could only see a murky profile because of the darkness, but whether it was the absence of light, or the drinks she'd consumed, when she looked at him she suddenly wondered what it would be like to kiss his full lips. She traced the outline of them with her eyes and found herself biting down hard on her own lip as she imagined it.

"Oh my god, snap out of it," she told herself, closing her eyes and shaking her head.

"Sorry?"

"Nothing."

"Right. So is it your mother or you who is interested in me? I'm confused."

"Neither of us and you know it."

"I don't know anything when it comes to you Maggie Tanner," he took his eyes off the road again and studied her. "But I'd love the opportunity to find out."

For once she had no retort, so she leant her head back and closed her eyes again, pretending to doze off. When she knew his attention was back on the road she let her eyes open. She watched his hand as he expertly flicked through the gears. He had large hands, broad across the top and with long fingers. She remembered when those fingers had connected with hers and the jolt she'd felt. God why was she even thinking of things like this? She squeezed her eyes shut and turned her head towards the window. It was all Harpers fault, with all her talk of sex and how long it had been.

The sound underneath the tyres changed and she realised they had turned onto the gravel road. She felt disappointment that the ride was over so soon.

"We're here," he said softly, pulling up to the front of the house and turning off the engine.

She pretended to wake from her snooze and yawned, stretching.

"I suppose I should say thank you."

"That's what normal people do, yes."

"Thanks." She said the word reluctantly.

"You're welcome."

She got out of the car and was two steps towards the house when she heard footsteps behind her. She whirled around and came smack up against his chest.

"And where do you think you're going?" she demanded.

He sighed. "I was seeing you safely to your door. It's what a gentleman does."

"As if *you* would know *anything* about gentlemanly behaviour."

"Now see, I resent that. You haven't even given me a chance to show you any of my various charms."

The way he said it the words came out loaded like sexual innuendo bullets. He was standing so close she could feel his breath again, hot on her face. The smell of his cologne warmed by his body was enveloping her. She knew she couldn't think straight when she was so close to him but still she didn't step away. Instead she decided to play him at his own game and she stepped even closer, letting her own heady mix of sweet body smells mingle with his. Earthy Sandalwood and sweet vanilla combined together and created a haze that swirled around them.

"You think you're so irresistible, don't you?" she whispered, looking up at him from under her eyelashes. She bit one corner of her lip seductively.

He groaned gently. "You're driving me crazy," he whispered.

"And how am I doing that?"

"You know exactly how," he fired back, his eyes boring into hers. "You've woven some kind of spell on me and I can't get you out of my head."

Maggie laughed softly, "I've done no such thing."

"Then why is your face the first thing I picture when I wake, and the last thing I think about when I try to go to sleep. Why do I lie there half the night, awake, tossing and turning and imagining what it would be like to kiss you, to touch you."

Maggie swallowed. This wasn't a game anymore. His eyes were serious, and the way they searched probingly into hers made her body want to relax against him and let him soothe all her troubles away.

"We can't do this," she said.

"Do what?" he whispered, his face dipping towards hers, his lips gently brushing over her forehead then her cheeks, tantalising and teasing her skin and her senses. She could hold back no longer and she reached up with her hands and pulled his head down towards hers hungrily. They kissed long and hard, not a gentle movie star kiss, rather something primal, lots of gnashing teeth, tongues and bruised lips, as if they were trying to clamber as far inside each other as they could.

Maggie had forgotten just how wonderful a really good kiss could be.

Finally they were forced to break for breath, and with the inhale of cool air Maggie remembered where she was, and realised what she was doing and who she was doing it with. How could she want someone so much when he drove her insane almost every time she saw him?

He reached for again but she pushed him away. "No, stop."

He paused. "What's wrong?"

"We can't do this."

"Why not?"

And for the life of her she couldn't think of a satisfactory answer for that question. So she gave in and let him pull her back in for more. Minutes later it was he who pulled away.

"No," he said, holding her out at arm's length.

"What's wrong?"

"We can't do this."

"Why not?" She was angry he was throwing her words back at her when she had so successfully overcome them.

"You've been drinking, I don't want you to wake up tomorrow and think I took advantage."

She stamped a foot. "How many times must I tell you I'm not drunk."

He sighed and shuddered as longing ran its fingers lightly down his spine.

"Still," he said, "you have been drinking."

"I know how to prove it to you," she declared. "Hold up one finger."

Amused, he did as she instructed.

"Now," she said. "Ask me how many fingers you're holding up."

He laughed.

"Go on, ask me," she insisted.

147

"How many fingers am I holding up?" he asked, amused. He had become accustomed to her being so serious all the time, so to see this lighter side was refreshing.

"One," she declared triumphantly. "Just one. Now if I was drunk would I be able to see straight like that?"

"I get the feeling you might have cheated," he laughed again, pulling her back in against him, enjoying the way her body slotted in against his like two pieces of a jigsaw puzzle.

"Never," she shook her head, "I'm as straight up as they come."

He stepped back slightly and looked her up and down.

"Straight up? Looks to me like you go in and out in quite a few interesting places."

She groaned. "Don't ruin this moment by saying corny crap like that."

"Corny? I'll have you know my charms go down a treat with the ladies back in the big smoke."

"Well us country girls are a little more discerning."

He touched her bottom lip with his fingers, marvelling at the dark ruby colour his kiss had left it.

"I thought you hated me," he said.

"Hate is a strong word."

"So you don't hate me?" he bit her lip ever so gently.

She moaned and pressed against him. God this felt insanely good, better than she'd ever remembered. She couldn't stop now. Why not give in and let herself have one night of fun? Prove to Harper and the others that she wasn't completely against letting loose once in awhile. Who would it hurt? Not a soul, that's who. They were both consenting adults. Consenting, turned on adults. Why deprive themselves?

"Come with me," she told him, taking his hand and leading him up the steps.

He pulled her hand and stopped her. She turned to him.

"Are you sure about this?" he asked, "completely, one hundred percent, not-going-to-regret-it in the morning sure?"

She dropped his hands and peeled her top off over her head as an answer, dropping it to the deck beside her.

"Just fun," she breathed huskily. "No strings attached, right?"

He gulped at the black lacy bra and expanse of skin now available for his viewing pleasure.

"God you're so beautiful," he said, his voice hungry with desire.

She was enjoying the feeling of power she had, the reckless abandon the night air and a few drinks had afforded her. She put her hands on her hips and pouted at him.

"So are you coming inside or not?"

He raised his eyebrows at her double entendre, whether it was intended or not.

"Oh most definitely," he said. "Lead the way gorgeous."

"Shhh," Maggie whispered at the door, a finger to her lips. Then she giggled. She felt like she was fifteen and sneaking a boy home. Inside they crossed the living room swiftly, heading for Maggie's room at the back of the house, their desire leaving a crimson streak of phosphorous air in their wake.

In the kitchen, Dot stood frozen, melted into the shadows in the corner. She had been at the fridge looking for something to snack on when she'd heard their voices at the front door. Quickly shutting the fridge to cut the light, she'd stepped back into the corner so they wouldn't see her. Not that she needed have bothered. She could have stood in a spotlight banging a drum and wearing a silver space suit for all the notice they gave their surroundings. She could feel the heat of their desire from over where she stood.

"Phew-ey," she said, fanning her face with one hand and grinning. Sometimes her meddling landed her in trouble. Sometimes, like tonight, it paid off. She waited until she heard Maggie's door close then she headed up the stairs to her own room, checking on Willow as she passed. Willow was sound asleep, hair splayed across her pillow, her mouth slightly open and air whistling softly between her teeth. Dot kissed her on the forehead and pulled her blanket back up over her shoulders.

"Sleep tight, sweet girl. When you wake up your mother's going to be a new woman."

She grinned again at the thought.

Back in her own bed, she had just nestled down when there was a muffled thud and a crash like something had been smashed downstairs. Beside her Ray sat bolt upright in his bed.

"What was that?" he growled, starting to throw back the covers and reaching under the bed where he kept a cricket bat.

"Hush old man," Dot reassured him, a hand on his shoulder to coax him back into bed. "It's nothing for you to worry about, I promise. Go back to sleep."

Chapter thirteen

"Mum, Gran wants to know if you're planning on joining us for breakfast today."

Willow's voice hollering through her closed door roused Maggie from the deep slumber she'd been happily dwelling in. She murmured and stretched, briefly wondering why her body felt like she'd just done three straight hours of yoga.

"Morning sunshine," a voice said softly into her air. It was a satisfied voice, practically purring.

Her eyes flew open.

Memories came flooding back.

Oh god, she thought. What have I done?

"I'll be out in a minute baby, you start without me," she called to Willow, squeezing her eyes shut and scrambling to cover herself with the top sheet. When she was happy that no parts of her were showing that shouldn't be, she inched off the bed sideways and took a deep breath.

"Are you decent?" she asked.

"That depends what you mean by decent."

"Dammit Jack, you know exactly what I mean."

"Then yes. I am decent."

She opened her eyes. He *was* decent, but only just. Before she could stop them her eyes traced a line from his broad arms, currently crossed behind his head on the pillow, down his sinewy torso to where his stomach dipped into a concave and disappeared beneath the sheet.

"Oh my god," she said, covering her face with her hands then pulling them away again to yank up the sheet that had started to drop. "I can't believe we…"

"Yep," he grinned, "three times."

"Shut up."

He rolled over onto his side, propping his head up on one hand. "You promised me you wouldn't regret it."

"I don't," she said, happy to realise she meant it. "But I'd prefer last night wasn't spoken of again."

He frowned. "That will make it hard for me to tell the guys at the pub about it."

"You wouldn't dare," she protested, then realised he was joking. "Oh ha ha," she picked up her pillow and threw it at him. He reached up to catch it and his sheet slipped even lower. He noticed the direction of her eyes.

"How about a repeat," he suggested, "for old time's sakes?"

And Maggie had to shake herself when she realised she had paused to consider it.

'No," she said loudly. With a nervous glance at the door she lowered her voice in case the others heard her. "You have to leave."

He sighed. "But I don't want to."

"Please," she pleaded. "I really don't want Willow to know about this."

He understood her concern was only for her daughter. "Ok," he said. "But how will I get past without them seeing me?"

Maggie searched around the room for an answer. "The window," she said triumphantly. "You can go out the window."

"Are you serious?"

"*Please*."

"I have to say this element of danger is getting me somewhat excited again."

"Down tiger," she threw his clothes at him. "Quick, get dressed before Willow comes back. It's not like her to just knock, next time she might just come barging in."

Maggie turned away while Jack pulled on his jeans and T-shirt. She opened the curtains and the blinding sun that flooded the room left them in no doubt that today was going to be another scorcher. The house had old sash windows, the kind you lifted to open. Over the years the ropes that worked the pulley system had aged and sometimes need a little extra persuasion to work. Maggie pounded at one corner of the window to unstuck it.

"Come on you stupid thing," she muttered, and then said "aha," as it came free and she could lift it.

"Right," she turned to Jack. "Go."

"That's it?"

"What?"

He sat down on the corner of the bed. "How about a goodbye kiss, or simply thanks for the ride last night. The one in the car I meant," he added hurriedly when he saw her face.

"Thank you for the lift home. Now please get up and go, before my daughter comes back and sees you."

"Ok ok. But when can I see you again?"

"Oh no you don't," she shook her finger at him. "Last night was a one off, remember? We agreed; no strings attached. Don't you start getting soppy on me."

"I'm fairly sure that's normally the guy's line."

She flicked an anxious glance at the door. "What will it take for me to get you to leave?"

"A promise to see me again soon. For dinner, or coffee or a walk. Your choice."

"Ok, I'll call you."

"Good." He smiled and crossed to the window. Looking outside he realised there was a thorny rose bush underneath her window. He raised her eyebrows at her.

"Sorry," she said. "Dad planted it there when I was a teenager to prevent just this sort of thing. You're the first who has ever had to risk it though."

155

"You owe me two dates for this," he muttered, one leg over the windowsill and pausing while he tried to judge where the best landing place was.

"Mum," there was a knock on the door and then the door knob rattled as it was turned. Without thinking Maggie shoved Jack then turned to stand in front of the window, just as her daughter came into the room. There was a muffled swear word from the garden outside and Maggie coughed to cover it.

"What's taking you so long?" Willow asked suspiciously. "And were you talking to someone?"

"No, just singing to welcome in the new day," Maggie lied brightly, "la la la di la, etc. Did you want something?"

Willow walked over to her mother and looked her up and down.

"Why are you only wearing a sheet? And why is your face all red like that?"

"Christ Willow, what's with the interrogation? I'm just flushed because I did a few yoga exercises, that's all."

"Wearing a sheet?"

"Yes, Willow, wearing a sheet. Now go and finish your breakfast, I'll be out in a minute." Willow walked away, but at the door she turned and regarded her mother sceptically.

'You're up to something," she said. "And I'm going to figure out what."

Then she left.

Maggie exhaled and turned back to the window. There was no sign of Jack. She sank down on to the bed. Phew. What a night. Upon reflection, she had no regrets at all. It had been a thoroughly enjoyable night; at least that's what her body was telling her. She had a feeling she might not be thinking the same later in the day though when muscles that hadn't been used in sometime started to protest their sudden use. It was the deception and adrenaline rush she'd just had that she could do without, her heart was still pounding from the fear of getting caught.

She quickly showered, using her parsley soap to help ward off any potential hangover, and threw on a long yellow summer dress. The day was already hot and seconds out of the shower she felt a trickle of sweat make its way down between her shoulder blades. She stopped by her shop room to flick on the air conditioner then headed out to the kitchen. Already, as per her earlier premonition, parts of her body were starting to make their protests known. It had been a fun night, she admitted to herself, but despite her promise to get Jack out of the window she had no intention of seeing him anytime soon. So when she rounded the corner and saw him sitting at the kitchen table her mouth dropped open and she stopped dead in her tracks.

What the hell was he playing at?

He looked at her sheepishly.

"Morning" sang Dot from the stove where she was transferring bacon from a hot frying pan to a plate. "You're just in time for breakfast. And look who's joined us."

"Morning," said Jack.

"I found him outside," said Ray, "claims he was out walking his dog."

"Yep, just out for another early morning walk with Rufus. Best way to start the day I find," replied Jack in an overly cheerful manner.

"Funny thing is, I didn't see any sign of the dog," Ray helped himself to some bacon.

Jack's mouth gaped comically while he searched for a suitable retort. Finding none in his sleep deprived brain, he shut his mouth and shrugged. "He's somewhere around."

Willow frowned at him. "You lost Rufus?"

"Of course not. He's not *lost,* as such. In fact I'm pretty sure he knows exactly where he is. I'll run into him again at some point."

Maggie looked down quickly to hide a smile. God help me, she thought, his humour is growing on me.

"Whatever weirdo," Willow pushed her chair out from the table.

'Lift it, don't scrape it."

She headed out to the front porch and Maggie didn't even consider where she was going until she was back a minute later, her head tilted to one side and her hands behind her back.

"That's weird," she said.

"What's weird baby?" Maggie asked, reaching over to grab herself a piece of toast from the freshly buttered pile.

"Dad didn't leave any meat last night."

Maggie's hand froze and her eyes widened in horror. She looked quickly from her mother to her father but they both avoided her gaze. How could she have forgotten? She knew exactly how, she'd been too busy enjoying herself. This was exactly why she'd avoided complications like men all these years, she thought furiously. She let her guard down for one minute and what had happened? She'd forgotten something so crucial.

"Really?" she finally said, selecting a piece of toast and trying to sound as normal as possible. Still, she could hear a quiver in her voice nevertheless.

"Yes, really. Do you think he's ok?"

"I'm sure he's fine, he probably just got caught up with something. Or maybe he had no luck hunting this week."

"I doubt it. He's never missed a week before."

"Everyone has their off days Willow. Don't worry about it, I'm sure next week he'll be back like normal."

"You don't think we ought to try and find him? Make sure he's ok?"

Maggie finally looked at her daughter. There was something in her voice that didn't quite sit right, like she was testing her mother. "No," she said firmly. "I'm sure he's fine."

Willow held her mother's gaze steadily for ten seconds, her eyes probing, and then she relaxed. "Ok," she said. "If you say so. Can I go see Nick?"

Maggie started to relax. It seemed she had gotten away with it, although it had been a close call. "Have you done all your homework?"

"Yep," Willow lied smoothly. It wasn't a complete lie, she had done *most* of her homework. The last bit she figured she could copy off Nick in the morning before the bell rang. Heck, as far as she was concerned they shouldn't even *have* homework in the last week of school, stupid sadist teacher, so he was lucky she'd bothered to do any at all.

"Ok then. But be home by lunchtime, and be safe."

Willow turned to go and Maggie allowed herself to relax and take a gulp from her coffee, but then Willow turned back quickly as if something else had just occurred to her.

"Oh and Mum?"

"Mmm?"

"Why was your top lying out on the front porch?"
Willow's hand came out from behind her back and held the
offending top up in front of her.

Maggie spat her coffee out and had a coughing attack.
Ray pounded her on the back while her face turned bright red.

"Alright dad, enough," she finally managed to splutter
as her colour returned to normal. He stopped smacking her.

"I must have dropped it there when I was bringing the
washing in yesterday," she said, thinking up the lie quickly.

"But Gran bought the washing in yesterday. And isn't
this the top you were wearing when you went out?"

"What's with you and all the questions this morning?"
Maggie snapped. "Sometimes things are just none of your
business ok?"

Willow looked hurt and tears sprang to her eyes.
Without another word she dropped the top on the floor and ran
out the front door. As she left they heard a small sob. She
hadn't heard that tone from her mother before, at least not
directed at her.

"Oh nice one Maggie," Dot sighed. "The poor girl has
done nothing wrong; she didn't deserve to be spoken to like
that."

"I know," Maggie dropped her head into her hands and
moaned.

"Well don't take *your* mistakes out on her. You were the one who forgot to put the meat out, and you were the one who left your top there for her to find. She's not a baby anymore; you can't blame her for being curious."

"I know mum, like I don't feel bad enough already?"

"Go after her and apologise"

"She'll be long gone by now. I'll sit down and have a talk with her later."

"Are you going to finally tell her the truth? Stop all this craziness for once and for all?"

"I don't know mum, ok? I don't know what I'm going to say."

"Ahem," Jack cleared his throat.

Maggie jumped, she had completely forgotten he was there. "Shit," she swore, "how much of that did you hear?"

"Well," he was confused by the question, "all of it, obviously. I mean, I am sitting right here and I'm not deaf."

"Well don't start asking questions. It really *is* none of your business."

He held up his hands defensively. "I wasn't going to ask anything."

"Good."

"Except maybe just *one* question —"

Maggie glared at him. "What?"

"Does your ex-husband really stop by every Saturday night to leave dead meat on your porch? Cause if he does, that's kind of creepy."

"Don't be so stupid, of course he doesn't."

"So why does Willow think he does?"

"That's two questions, and it's complicated."

"It's not complicated, it's stupid," said Ray.

"Gee thanks for the support dad."

"Honey, I support you all the way, you know that. But not when it comes to this. You should have told that girl the truth a long time ago."

"And the truth is what exactly?" asked Jack, looking around the table.

"None of your business," said Maggie.

"Yep, that's what I thought you'd say. You're making it all sound very mysterious. I mean, is there a body buried in the backyard that I should know I about?"

"Of course not. Don't say stupid things like that."

"Well if you don't want me to use my imagination then why not tell me the truth? Who delivers the meat? Where is Willow's father?"

Maggie stood up angrily.

"Lift it, don't scrape it."

"Outside," she ordered Jack, "*now.*"

"You'd better do what she says," Ray said, "she's got her bossy voice on."

Maggie stalked out the back door letting the screen slam shut behind her. The fern on the windowsill curled up its fronds defensively as she passed. Ray grimaced. "Yep, you're in trouble alright. I'd hate to be in your shoes."

Jack whistled out his breath. "Any tips you can give me that might help me survive this?"

"And take away all the fun? Nope, you're on your own," Ray grinned.

"Don't be so mean," Dot smacked him lightly on the back of the head. She turned to Jack and regarded him, one hand on her hip. She looked him up and down and then nodded. "I think you'll be fine. You've already proved you can hold your own with her in an argument, and that's half the battle right there. Just don't back down. She needs someone like you in her life; she just doesn't know it yet. Maggie can be a little stubborn you see, thinks she can do everything on her own. You didn't hear any of that from me though."

"You'd better go," Ray butted in. "The longer you leave her out there on her own the angrier she'll get."

Jack gulped and stood up.

"Lift it, don't scrape it."

"Wish me luck," he said.

"It's been nice knowing you," replied Ray cheerfully.

Outside Jack couldn't see Maggie at first, but he could hear muttered cursing so he followed the sound around the back of the house. She was bent over one of the raised vegetable beds, plucking out weeds furiously and throwing them on the ground to stomp on.

"You're busy," said Jack, turning to retreat, "I'll catch up with you later."

"*Get back here.*"

Jack winced, and turned slowly back towards her, plastering a broad smile across his face.

"What's up?" he asked.

"What's up? *What's up?* Are you kidding me?"

"Look, you're clearly upset. Maybe we should have this talk later."

"It's *you* that I'm upset at, and we are having this talk right now."

"Right. Ok."

She walked towards him jabbing one finger in his direction. "If you think for one minute that what happened last night entitles you to any kind of say in my life, you're mistaken."

"Oh no, I would never –"

The finger did an about turn and pointed at her. "*My* business is *my* business, and my daughter and I are none of *your* business, you got that?"

"Of course, I was just –"

"And that goes for my parents as well. Don't use them to try and find out things about me."

"I haven't," he protested, "I wouldn't –"

"What happened last night was -," she flicked a glance towards the house to make sure her parents weren't listening and lowered her voice, "- *sex,* and just sex. Nothing else, you got me? Don't go thinking it was an invitation to start asking questions about things that just don't concern you."

He stayed silent this time, simply stood still and watched her.

"*Body buried in the backyard?* What the hell is wrong with you? Imagine if Willow had heard you say that? Joking or not, it was in poor taste, but then you seem to say whatever the hell pleases you and who cares if it hurts someone else right?"

He frowned.

"I don't know why you feel this need to hunt out my past," she continued, "but I want you to stop."

Maggie finally ran out of steam and stopped talking, waiting for him to say something. He didn't.

"Aren't you going to say something?" she asked.

"Sorry, I wasn't sure if you were finished. Am I allowed to speak now?"

"Briefly, yes."

"Right, my turn," he said. His tone was low and even, and it startled her because she hadn't heard him speak so seriously before. "I don't know why you keep secrets the way you do or what it is that makes you think your experiences are any more traumatic than anyone else's, but here's the thing; your husband left you. It's as simple as that. No big drama, no scandal, no mystery. He just left you, as men leave women all the time and vice versa. It's one of those things that happen in life, as sad as it is when there are kids involved. I'm sure it's been happening for centuries and it will probably happen for centuries to come."

"How did you -?"

"Find out? Oh it wasn't hard, not in a small town like this. I ran into some of your mother's friends and they were more than happy to fill me in, without me having to ask a single leading question I might add. Seems your mother and her friends think you and I could be quite good together, something I agreed with right up until about now, when I realised what a major pain in the ass you actually are. You think I'm arrogant and maybe that's the case, but *you* are a judgmental shrew. You've been judging me since the day we met, and based on nothing. I thought after last night we were getting somewhere, but you're still determined to keep me at arm's length and play the grieving, mysterious victim. Wake up Maggie, you're the only one making yourself that. Your ex is the one who lost out, *he's* the one with the problem. If he knew how often you still think of him he'd be over the moon I'm sure. Forget it. Let it go.

Stop being angry at every man you meet and live life again, before you become so bitter and twisted your daughter ends up the same way."

Maggie gasped as if he had slapped her.

"Get out," she hissed. "Get off my land and get away from my family."

He shook his head. "I'm sorry things had to end this way. I really like you and I hoped maybe we could have had something. I hope you heed my words Maggie. Leave the past where it belongs and let it go. If you decide you want to live for the present and embrace life again, call me."

Then he was gone. She waited till she heard his truck start and crunch off down the driveway before she sank down onto the grass and dropped her head into her hands. She started to cry.

In the downstairs bathroom, Ray and Dot had been jostling for viewing space out the small slated window, taking turns to kneel on the closed toilet seat.

"Oh my baby," Dot said sadly. "I'd better go out to her."

"No," Ray put a hand on her arm. "He's right. Everything he said was right and she needed to hear it. Give her some time to absorb what she's heard. Maybe he'll finally get through to her where we've failed."

"I hope you're right."

"Only time will tell."

Outside, Maggie finished crying; using her long skirt to wipe the salty tears off her cheeks and chin where they had pooled and were hanging perilously.

"He has no idea what he's talking about," she sniffed to herself. She looked up at the house; if she knew her parents well enough, which she considered she did, they had been watching and eavesdropping on the whole exchange. She wondered why her mother hadn't come out to defend her, or commiserate with her because of all the horrible, untrue things Jack had said.

Because they *were* untrue.

Weren't they?

She lay down on the grass, squeezing her eyes shut against the bright glare of the sun. The grass tickled at the back of her legs and bare feet.

She didn't really act like a victim did she? She had worked so hard to provide for herself and Willow since Jon left, refusing to be reliant on anyone else. Were those the actions of a victim? No, they weren't.

Then the thought occurred to her; maybe he'd meant emotionally.

Was she an emotional victim? To her growing horror, she found she couldn't deny it. Oh my god, she thought. No. He can't be right.

But maybe, just maybe, he was.

She thought about all the passion she'd invested into hating Jon for what he'd done, for all those years. Energy wasted on a man who had never bothered to get back in touch, not even for his daughters sake. She thought of all the times she'd turned down dates, using her daughter as an excuse. And not just with men. Other gatherings, special occasions, all politely turned down by her because she didn't want to go and be the subject of anyone's pity, the woman whose husband couldn't stand her so much that he'd never contacted his own child again.

She'd blamed herself all this time.

But it *wasn't* her fault. It was *his* fault. *He* was the one with the problem. He was the one who left. He was the one who was a bad parent; not her. Yet here she was, with all these hang ups, refusing to let anyone close again in case she discovered they too thought she wasn't worth sticking around for. Jon had left her feeling unlovable. He'd left her aching with pain and guilt and the belief that it was her fault Willow had no father in her life; that she had driven him away.

She had to stop blaming herself for that.

It was *his* decision to leave. It was *his* decision to never come back and to never contact them again.

But it hurt. It hurt so, so much that they hadn't been enough for him. She was strong enough to take it, but was Willow?

She hadn't even realised that she'd been crying again, until a tear found its way into her ear and tickled as it slipped into her ear canal, causing her to give a little shudder. She sat up and dabbed her ear with her dress. It was peaceful out in the back garden. The grass could do with a mow, but it wasn't so long it was unsightly. Instead it waved in a barely perceptible breeze, and felt like a soft cool rug. Birds were singing, the sun was warm on her skin. Her mother had been right; summer and its bountiful days were just around the corner. She saw white butterflies hovering over the cabbages in the garden, so she got to her feet and picked up the old badminton racket leaning against a fence post. She waved it around to chase them away just as she had as a child. She closed her eyes and turned her face up to the sun and she smiled.

Life is good, she told herself.

Life is really, *really,* good.

And in that instant she made the decision to let go of her lingering hurt from the past. She might have thought she was doing the best she could for herself and Willow, but as long as she continued to harbour resentment and bitterness she would never truly be at peace. And oh, she longed for peace. She would focus on the here and now and enjoy each day as it came. But most importantly, she would forgive Jon. It was time to banish him from occupying so many of her thoughts.

And it was time to come clean to Willow. But first she had to find her.

Chapter fourteen

It wasn't too hard in the end. She called in at Nick's house but he informed her that even though he'd been expecting Willow to come round she hadn't shown up. Maggie knew he wasn't lying because his lip stayed unbitten and his ears a normal, healthy shade of pink.

"What did you do to upset her?" he shrewdly asked Maggie.

"Nick," his mother snapped, mortified. "Sorry Maggie," she apologised.

"It's ok," Maggie smiled. "If she shows up will you please give me a call?"

"Of course," said Nick's mum.

However Nick shook his head. "Depends whether she wants to talk to you or not."

"*Nick!*" His mother snapped again. She gave him a little shove. "Sorry Maggie," she apologised again.

"No its fine, really," Maggie assured her. "I admire his loyalty to my daughter."

She paused at the end of their driveway as she considered where she should look for her daughter next. Then the answer came to her and she smiled and turned left.

She could hear the babbling of the creek long before
she saw it, and the sound bought back memories of her own
childhood days spent fishing or swimming in this same spot.
Leaving her shoes by the car she hitched her dress into her
knickers and made her way carefully down the bank. Her
daughter was laying on her stomach, leaning out over the side
of the creek, her fingers trailing in the water. Maggie could hear
her sniffing as she approached and her heart broke that she had
made her precious daughter cry.

"I'm sorry baby," she said softly as she sat down beside
her. "Forgive me?"

In reply Willow burrowed her head into her mother's
lap, weaving her arms around her waist. She carried on sniffing
but didn't speak.

"I'm so sorry I snapped at you like that. You didn't do
anything wrong, I was just in a grumpy mood and I took it out
on you."

"Were you mad at Jack?" Willow finally spoke, her voice
muffled. She kept her face down.

"Why would you think that?"

"Because you always seem to be mad at him."

Maggie was surprised that Willow had been so
perceptive, although in hindsight she hadn't done such a great
job of hiding her feelings.

"A little bit," she admitted. "But mostly I was mad at myself."

"Why?"

Maggie sighed. This was the part she had been dreading.

She swept her daughters hair gently away from her face. "Look at me baby," she said. Willow sat up and wiped her nose on the back of her hand. Her eyes were puffy and red from crying.

Maggie took a deep breath. "Your father didn't leave us to live in the forest."

"He didn't?"

"No."

"So where does he live?"

"Honestly? I have no idea."

"Oh." Willow tilted her head while she digested this information.

"There's something else." Maggie closed her eyes, took a deep breath then opened them again. She didn't want to see the heartbreak on her daughters face, but as her mother she owed it to her to be honest. Finally.

"I haven't heard anything from your father since the day he left. The meat we get every weekend, it doesn't come from him." She scanned her daughters face anxiously, but was puzzled to see the news didn't seem to have affected her.

"Willow?"

Willow nodded. "I know."

"You know what?"

"That the meat doesn't come from dad."

"How do you -?"

"I stayed up late one night, years ago, and hid behind the long curtains in the lounge. I wanted to see what he looked like because I couldn't remember him. He never came, but I saw you go out to the freezer in the garage and get a chicken which you put in the chilly bin on the porch. I thought maybe you were just helping him out but then I sat up the next Saturday and the same thing happened, and the Saturday after that. I realised it was you all along. It's the same way I found out you and Gran are Santa Claus."

Maggie was astonished. "Why didn't you ever say anything?"

Willow shrugged. "I figured you had your reasons."

"So all this time I thought I was protecting you, and you already *knew*?"

"Yep. Protect me from what?"

Maggie drew her daughter in close again, enjoying the smell and the feel of her hair. She kissed her on the top of her head, remembering how she had kissed the same exact spot when her daughter was just a minute old. She felt something inside her scrunch up with the memory of the love that had flooded her body in that instant and which had only grown stronger with time.

"I didn't want you to think that your father left because of you. He loved you. He loved you so much, he really did. It was something between me and him that just broke and no matter how hard we tried we couldn't fix it. That's why he left."

"But if he loves me why doesn't he call? Or visit?"

Maggie was so tempted to lie; to make something up that would cushion any hurt. But she had promised herself she would only tell her daughter the truth from now on.

"I don't know," she admitted. "I really don't. But whatever reason he has, it's his loss. He's the one who is missing out on seeing what a wonderful, clever, beautiful young woman you're blossoming into."

"Oh god, don't be so embarrassing, mum," Willow ducked her head and blushed, but she smiled as she did so.

"I mean it. Every day I look at you and I feel blown away with how mature you're becoming. You're a really amazing girl, you know that?"

"Thanks mum. But seriously, you can shut up now."

Maggie laughed and squeezed her daughter tight.

"So what happens if he comes back one day and wants to see us?" Willow's face turned serious again.

"It's possible of course, and if he does we'll cross that bridge when we get to it. I would never stop you from seeing him, if it's what you wanted."

"I don't know what I'd want." Willow looked down into the water again. "It's really hard to miss someone when you don't remember them."

"I know."

"Mum?"

"Mm?"

"I never -," Willow struggled to find the words to express what she wanted to say. "I mean, I always felt loved, you know? I never felt I was missing out on anything, not having a dad here. You're the best mum in the world. And gran and granddad are pretty cool, most of the time."

Maggie laughed.

"I'm just trying to say that I love you, and I appreciate everything you do for me."

"Oh I love you too my sweet little girl," Maggie gave an emotional sob and squeezed her daughter in for another hug.

"Ouch mum, you're going to crack a rib if you squeeze any harder."

"Sorry."

"Mum?"

"Yes?"

"You need to stop treating me like a little kid. I'm going to be eleven next year remember? You don't have to keep hiding things from me just because you think I need protecting."

"You're absolutely right," Maggie nodded.

"So you'll treat me more like an adult?"

"Well, how about more like a teenager. I don't want you to grow up too quickly."

"Ok deal."

Maggie released her and got to her feet, holding out a hand. "Come on you, we'd better get home. I want to check that homework you say you've done."

Willow pulled a face. "About that –"

"Hmm, that's what I thought."

Willow put her hand in her mothers, and as Maggie pulled her up she dipped her hand into the cold creek and flicked water at her mother's face.

"Ooh you little toad," Maggie gasped as the cold droplets touched her sun warmed skin.

Willow laughed and darted out of reach, heading up the bank towards the car.

"Serves you right for lying to me for so long," she called back over her shoulder.

"It wasn't a lie so much as simply an extension of the truth," Maggie followed her.

"That's just a fancy way of saying it was bullshit."

"Don't swear, but yes, that's correct."

On the drive home they were quiet, each caught in their own thoughts. Maggie was reflecting on how different everything suddenly seemed. The world, in general, had brightened by at least three shades. She certainly felt as if a burden had been banished from her body. She felt carefree and excited about this new relationship with her daughter, one where there were no more secrets between them.

"Mum, is there something going on between you and Jack?"

Well maybe just *one* secret.

"No. Why?"

"I think he likes you."

Maggie took her eyes off the road for a second and looked at her daughter. "Why do you think that?"

"Eyes on the road mum, that's what you always tell granddad."

"Sorry." It seemed her daughter had been paying attention to her all these years after all.

"Just the way he looks at you."

"And how does he look at me?"

"Like you're an ice block on a hot day and he's really thirsty."

Maggie swallowed a laugh. Willow had hit the nail on the head with her description. "I think you might be right."

"So?"

"So what?"

"Duh, so do you like him too?"

"I don't know," Maggie crinkled her nose up. "Sometimes maybe. But then other times I feel like he's the most annoying person on the planet." It felt weird, but nice, to be talking about something like this with her daughter. A prelude to the future of their relationship. She felt a twinge of nostalgia for the little girl she was losing.

"Josie Smith says that's what true love is."

"What?"

"When you hate someone so much but at the same time you can't imagine living without them."

"Hell. Josie Smith sounds freakishly mature."

"She reads her mother's books."

"What sort of books?"

"You know, books about to how keep a man, stuff like that."

"I think someone should tell Josie's mother to put those books higher out of reach."

"Don't *you* dare. Promise me."

"Ok, I promise."

"If you like Jack then you should see him."

"You wouldn't mind?"

"No. I think it will be nice for you to have someone else to focus your attention on apart from me."

"Is that a polite way of saying I smother you?"

"Yep. But I don't mind really. It's nice that you love me so much."

They pulled into their driveway and Maggie turned the engine off. Neither of them made a move to get out straight away. Maggie turned sideways in her seat and noticed for the first time how lanky her daughter was getting. Her long, tanned limbs were bony like they'd been stretched overnight. The hem on Willow's skirt had shot up about three inches too. New clothes were needed, Maggie realised. Lucky school was nearly finished and summer was almost here; Willow practically lived in her bathing suit through the warm months.

"So, we're good?" Maggie asked.

Willow smiled broadly, "we're good."

"Right, you go and get your books out while I grab the washing off the line. I'll be inside in a minute."

But when she walked into the house five minutes later, dumping the clothes on the couch to be folded up later, Willow was not sitting at the table with her books spread out in front of her. Instead, she was hopping up and down from foot to foot, her face an explosion of excitement. Dot was standing beside her, the two of them smiling hopefully at Maggie.

"What?" Maggie asked suspiciously.

"You've forgotten haven't you?" Dot said.

"I told you she had," sighed Willow. "But technically I'd forgotten as well."

"I'm not sure," Maggie answered slowly. "Why don't you remind me exactly what it is I'm supposed to have forgotten?"

"Carols by Candlelight. Tonight, at the Town Square. You promised Willow you would take her this year."

"Oh, right." Maggie vaguely remembered making such a promise, back in July when Christmas seemed a lifetime away. Blasted thing had a habit of sneaking up on you. "You don't really want to go do you baby?" she asked hopefully.

"Yeah mum, I do."

"But it's a Sunday night," Maggie pointed out. "What kind of idiot organises these things on a school night?"

"But mum," willow wailed, "it's the last week so it's not like I'll be learning anything anyway. All we do in the last week is clean the classroom and run around the field a million times while the teachers get drunk and swap presents in the staffroom."

Maggie raised her eyebrows and looked questioningly at Dot, who couldn't quite meet her gaze.

"Mum?" Maggie asked. "Where did she get that idea from?"

"How should I know? Probably something she saw on the TV."

"Yeah right." Maggie was tired and could really do without going into town, but her daughters face reminded her of her new pledge to live in the moment so she smiled. "Alright then, go and get ready. We'll grab something to eat in town."

"Yay thanks mum! You're the best," Willow ran over and hugged her quickly round the waist then thundered up the stairs to her room.

"Things are obviously ok between you two again," Dot said.

"Things are perfect actually. And just so you and Dad know and can stop hassling me about it, she knows the truth."

"Everything?"

"Everything."

Dot clapped her hands together in delight. "Wonderful," she declared. "This calls for a celebratory drink." She headed over to the cabinet they kept their liquor in and selected a bottle of whiskey.

"Ug, not for me thanks." Maggie shook her head. "My liver is begging me not to relive last night."

Dot smirked. "I bet other parts of you aren't complaining."

"Oh god mum, don't be so embarrassing."

"What? I'm just happy for you. It's about time. Jack is a really nice guy."

"He's ok," Maggie shrugged. "But whatever, doesn't matter. It's over before it even begun."

Dot frowned while pouring herself another measure of whiskey. "Why?"

"Don't tell me you didn't hear him this morning. I know you and dad would have been listening from somewhere."

"Oh right. That."

"He made it pretty clear what he thought of me."

"And what is that, exactly?"

"That I'm some kind of pathetic victim who is stuck in the past, obsessed with a drop kick of an ex-husband and who hates all men."

"That's not what I heard."

"Are you sure you were listening to the same conversation?"

"He may have said something along those lines," Dot admitted, "but that's not what he really thinks of you. Anyone with half a brain in their head can see he likes you. Why do you think he dropped everything to pick you up last night when I called?"

"I don't know, to humour you? For some reason he's got this idea in his head that you and dad are his new best friends."

"Oh that's sweet," Dot was chuffed.

"Don't be so pleased with yourself, I don't think he knows many other people in this town."

"He's a lovely man and you could do much worse."

"Just leave it mum. You didn't see the look he gave me when he left."

"You give up too easy, that's your problem right there."

"What do you want me to do? Beg him for another chance? I don't think so."

"Show him that what he said this morning helped, that you're ready for a fresh start."

"I don't know. Maybe last night was all Jack and I were ever supposed to have."

Dot threw back the last of her whiskey and murmured disapprovingly. "I didn't raise you to be a quitter, Maggie May Tanner."

"I'm not quitting mum, I'm just not going to make a fool of myself."

Back in her room though, she sat on the corner of her bed and put her head in her hands. Last night had been wonderful. It was the closest she'd been to another human in such a long time, and had reminded her just how soul nourishing contact like that could be. But when she thought about the way she'd spoken to him this morning, basically labelling him an obsessed stalker, she felt mortified. Was she so out of touch with the world of relationships that the minute someone showed interest in her she suspected them of ulterior motives and accused them of such?

She crossed the room and stood in front of the mirror. It wasn't something she indulged in, usually too busy to make an effort with make-up, and of course there hadn't been anyone lately that she'd wanted to make an effort for. She studied her face properly for the first time in a long time. She was surprised to see faint lines around the edges of her eyes. She smiled experimentally and was alarmed to see it made them worse. She decided it was time to start investing in a good anti-wrinkle cream, and also to start wearing sunscreen if she was going to be outside for any length of time. She might have blown her chances with Jack, but maybe next time someone else asked her out she might say yes for a change.

Jack.

She sighed.

She was still furious with him for the way he had spoken to her and the things he had said, even if he had been right. But when she thought of the way he'd looked at her on the porch last night she broke out in shivers.

"Mum I'm ready," she heard Willow call from out by the kitchen.

"Ok I'll be out in a minute," Maggie called back. She looked in the mirror again and decided that she had nothing to lose by making herself look as presentable as possible. Rummaging under the sink she came across some mineral powder foundation she'd bought years ago on a whim, and a mascara wand. The mascara was a little clumpy, but she added a drop of water to the bottle and it loosened up. The effect was subtle, but she liked it. Under the sink she also found a curling spray, and she scrunched it into the end of her hair and watched them bounce up into appealing ringlets. Throwing on a red dress and a black cardigan she took one last look in the mirror. Not bad, she smiled to herself, and the wolf whistles when she walked out to the kitchen confirmed it.

"Thanks guys," she smiled gratefully.

"Wow mum," admired Willow, "you look so different."

"Different good? Or different hideous."

"Good of course. You look really young and pretty."

"Why thank you my darling."

"She's right," Ray said, kissing her on the cheek. "You look very beautiful my dear."

"Thanks dad," she smiled gratefully. "Are you coming with us to the carols?"

"Like I have a choice?" he grumbled.

"Of course he's coming," Dot said firmly, pushing him from behind in the direction of the door. "He wouldn't miss it for the world."

As her parents and daughter argued over who would have the front seat Maggie watched them, feeling a deep flood of love expand her ribcage. They may be an odd bunch, she thought, but they were her everything.

Chapter fifteen

Lady Luck was on their side and they found a carpark down a side street just off Town Square and only a minutes walk away. Ray carried a picnic basket, Maggie a blanket and Willow carried the huge newspaper wrapped bundle of Fish 'n' Chips they had just picked up. Maggie was glad she'd had the foresight to call ahead and place an order, as it seemed everyone in town had the same idea for dinner. The shop had been packed with people waiting for orders but theirs had been ready and waiting so she'd only had to pay and collect.

As they walked the aroma soaked through the paper and caused their stomachs to growl hungrily; they couldn't wait to set up their blanket and rip open the bundle.

Town Square had been decorated again; this time in the spirit of Christmas. Tinsel had been woven around the Angel Oak's branches and fairy lights and Chinese lanterns were already ablaze. The air had that muted, hazy feel you often get with dusk in summer, like you're looking at the world through a soft focus. A stage was set up at one end for the carollers, and the Christmas manger set had been borrowed from the church and was set up to one side. In front of it a collection box had been placed to fundraise for a new manger. This one was going on fifteen years old and had been touched up with so many layers of paint that baby Jesus' head was about five times bigger than it should be, and, due to a mishap with the white paint one year, the sheep now looked decidedly pink.

As they passed it Dot elbowed Ray and told him to contribute. He reluctantly fished in one pocket for a gold coin and dropped it in the slot, grumbling about how he'd contributed enough over the years by paying taxes.

"Don't be such a cheapskate," Dot scolded.

They found a spare patch of grass from where they could easily see the stage and Maggie spread out the blanket. Ray had a bit of trouble folding his knees enough to get down but with a few grunts he managed it. Dot unpacked the picnic basket, pulling out paper plates, a bottle of tomato sauce, salt and some bread that she had already buttered back at home.

"Right," she announced. "We're ready."

"Open it?"

"Open it."

Willow carefully peeled back the layers of newspaper, releasing the delicious smell of battered fish and salty chips into the air. They'd also got a few crab sticks, hot dogs and corn fritters.

"Ohhh," they all sighed contentedly, eyeing the feast.

Ray grabbed a plate and piled it high and then he grabbed the bottle of sauce and upended it, squeezing a liberal amount over his food. Then he creakily got back to his feet.

"Where do you think you're going?" Dot asked him.

"If I sit on that hard ground for two hours you'll have to wheel me home in a wheelbarrow," he said, "I'm off to join the lads where it's more comfortable." Dot looked over his shoulder to where Sam, Fred and Trevor were sitting. They waved when they saw her looking and she waved back. Although she smiled at them she muttered at the same time through clenched teeth "Silly old men."

"Hey I don't insult your friends."

"Yes you do. Just yesterday you said, and I quote, 'tell those crazy old biddies to stop calling during my afternoon nap'. Remember?"

"Well, they woke me up twice this week," he complained.

"Whatever. Go and join your friends."

Ray left and the women tucked into their meal. As invariably happened whenever they treated themselves to fish 'n' chips, they all indulged far too much, and it wasn't long before the three of them were spread out on their backs on the blanket, hands on tummies, groaning with the effort it took to even speak.

"Oh my god I can't move," Maggie huffed.

"Me either," Dot moaned. "Willow, roll the leftovers back up in the newspaper so I don't have to look at them."

"Can't. Reach. You do it."

192

"You're younger and closer."

"Yeah, but you're rounder so can roll over easier."

"Cheeky girl," Dot swatted out ineffectually towards Willow, who arched her body out of reach.

"I'll do it," Maggie said, managing to sit up on the third try. Truth was, she was grateful for the opportunity to look around at the crowd. The local band were just starting to warm up their instruments ready to begin the carolling. Soon, twilight would set in and then it would be harder for her to spot people she knew in the crowd. Although there was only one person she hoped to spot, and that was Jack. She was hoping he had cooled off and would come to her to apologise, opening the way for her to explain why she'd acted the way she had. She figured he was most likely feeling pretty bad about how he had talked to her and she didn't want to make him suffer for too long. No, she would gracefully accept his apology and when he made his next comment about the two of them having dinner or catching a coffee, as he invariably would, she would pretend to consider it for a brief moment, and then she would accept.

"Willow, go and get us some song sheets and candles," Maggie said, handing her daughter a twenty dollar note. "One each is enough," she quickly added before her daughter had even taken a step. She knew Willow; she would think the candles and spend the whole twenty.

Sure enough, "Aw mum," Willow pouted.

"One each."

Willow returned five minutes and handed over the candles and song sheets. Dot quickly scanned it and exclaimed happily, "Oh they're playing all my favourites, how wonderful."

"See anyone we know?" Maggie asked Willow casually.

"Like who?"

"Like anyone we know, friends."

Willow shrugged. "Kids from school. Harper's over there somewhere," she pointed to the right.

"I'll go and say hi later." Maggie hid her disappointment.

The music started and they sang 'Silent Night' and 'Jingle Bells'. As they sang twilight deepened, and as the last notes of Good King Wenceslas fell away into the night air the Mayor, who was presenting, announced it was time to light the candles. Dot dug some matches out of the picnic basket and lit their three. All around them people did the same, and soon the Square looked like a blanket of stars, bright pin pricks against the inky night.

"It's so beautiful," Maggie said softly. She couldn't remember ever feeling so content. She could feel goodwill and cheer drifting all around them. She closed her eyes and breathed deep.

"Look mum, there's Jack."

Her eyes flew open again.

"Where?"

Dot gave her a knowing look.

"There. Jack," Willow called out. Maggie looked in the direction Willow was gazing direction, smile at the ready but then her heart skidded in her chest; he wasn't alone. There was a woman with him, someone she hadn't seen before. They were sitting on small deck chairs about six metres away, glasses of wine in hand, some food spread in front of them. They hadn't been there the last time Maggie looked so must have been late arrivals. The woman was in the middle of saying something to Jack and laughing, and when she finished he laughed along with her.

"Jack," Willow called again, louder, before Maggie had a chance to shush her. This time he heard and looked their way. His eyes connected with Maggie's and she smiled, but although he held her gaze for a few seconds he didn't smile back, merely nodded a greeting. Then he turned his gaze to the waving Willow and finally he smiled.

"Hey Willow, how's your night going?" he called.

"Good thanks," she called back, "although we ate far too much." She puffed out her cheeks and held her arms out like a barrel.

Jack laughed. "Was that your sweet voice I heard singing before?"

"Probably. I hope you're not planning on singing though. We might have to move if you do."

He laughed. "There's the Willow we all know and love. It unnerves me when you're nice."

"Willow, don't be so cheeky," Maggie scolded.

"Leave her be," said Dot.

"Evening Dot," Jack dipped his head.

"Evening Jack," she smiled back. "And who is your friend?"

"Mum," Maggie hissed at her mother's bluntness but Dot ignored her.

"This is Amy," Jack introduced. "Amy, meet Dot, Willow and Maggie."

Maggie waited for him to make further explanation, such as 'Amy here is my sister', or 'Amy is a friend from my book club', something, *anything* to signal there was nothing romantic between them, but he stayed silent.

"Well, it's lovely to meet you Amy," she said eventually.

"You too," smiled Amy. She was beautiful, with honey blond hair, startling green eyes the colour of jade, and a smile that was almost brighter than the candle she was holding. It was a genuine smile, open and honest, so as much as Maggie wanted to dislike her she found herself warming to her instead.

"You guys enjoy the rest of your evening," Jack said, in a tone that indicated conversation between them was now over.

"You too," Maggie mumbled. She turned away from Jack, her cheeks flaming. Who had she been kidding? No amount of makeup or curling spray could compete with the beautiful Amy. She wanted to pack up and go home, but Willow was watching her anxiously. She had sensed the atmosphere and was worried for her, Maggie realised. Yet another sign that her perceptive daughter was growing up.

"Are you ok mum?

"I'm fine baby," Maggie plastered on a smile. She drew her daughter close into a circle inside her legs and nestled her chin on top of her daughters head. "Are you warm enough?"

"I'm fine."

"Well I'm a little chilly, so is it ok if I hug you in public? Or are you are worried someone from school might see us."

Willow sighed theatrically. "Well, I do have a certain reputation to maintain, but just this once I'll make an exception." She snuggled back in against her mother.

They sang along to the carols, waving their candles and shaking them every now and then so the wax dripped off and didn't run down through the cardboard circle to burn their hands. Maggie tried really hard to ignore the fact that Jack was nearby with someone else, but it was like her eyes had a mind of their own, and every so often she felt them drag against her will to sneak a glance in his direction. She saw Amy laugh at something he'd said and place her fingertips lightly on his bare forearm, and Maggie was startled by the strong urge she felt to get up and rip the woman's hand from Jacks body. She felt proprietorial towards him, which was crazy because the whole time she'd known him she'd been basically telling him to get lost.

Willow felt her mother stiffen. "Are you sure you're ok mum? We can leave if you like."

Maggie kissed her on the top of her head, pressing her lips tightly against her daughter's hair. She would do anything to protect this kid.

"It's ok sweetheart, really. I'm fine. Let's enjoy the carols."

It finished just after eleven and ended with a fireworks display that made everyone go 'ooooh' and 'ahhhh' appreciatively. There was a minor hiccup when one of the rockets exploded out of its packaging sideways and made a beeline right for the bench seat where the old men were sitting passing a hip flask back and forth. Dot laughed so hard she had to cross her legs so she didn't wet herself.

"That's the fastest any of them have moved in years," she howled, tears streaming down her face.

"Way to show your concern mum," said Maggie, trying hard not to laugh herself. She glanced sideways at Jack and saw he was also enjoying the unexpected show.

"Time to go," Dot said.

"Pull me up," Maggie asked Willow, holding up her hands. Willow took her hands and pretended to huff and puff with the strain of helping her mother to her feet. Once up, Maggie picked up the basket and Dot folded the blanket, shaking a bit of loose grass off first.

"Do we have to go already?" pouted Willow, holding the leftover fish n chips wrapped in what was now soggy and cold newspaper.

"Yes we do," Maggie told her firmly, "you have school tomorrow miss, remember?"

"School ruins everything."

"Yeah yeah, we've heard it all before," Dot said, ushering her granddaughter along with a gentle hand on the back. "Coming?" she asked Maggie, who had stopped to linger. She was watching Jack and Amy, who were also packing up to leave. Jack folded the chairs effortlessly in one hand, and with the other placed in the small of Amy's back he steered her in the direction of his truck.

"Mm? I was just making sure we hadn't left anything," Maggie replied. She was amazed that her voice came out so level, when inside her emotions were whirling like a mini tornado, uprooting and damaging everything in their path.

She had been right and Jack was nothing but a fickle bastard after all, she thought angrily. How quickly had he found someone else once he'd decided that she was too much trouble and not worth the effort? Less than a day, that's all it took. She supposed that she should be grateful she'd found out the truth now before she'd made a fool of herself by letting him know she was actually interested. She wasn't going to let him see that sight of him with someone else bothered her, so she marched determinedly ahead, leaving Dot and Willow in her wake, and she caught up with Jack and Amy underneath the big Angel Oak tree.

"I can't believe how many lights there are, there must be hundreds," Amy was saying.

"Thousands probably," Jack answered.

"Surely it's a fire hazard?" Amy frowned, her pretty little forehead crinkling.

"I'm sure they know what they're doing, "Jack said, and then he leaned his head in closer to Amy's as if they were co-conspirators. "Although after the fireworks fiasco, maybe I'm giving them too much credit," he added.

There he goes again, insulting our town, Maggie thought angrily. Amy obviously felt the same way he did from the way she threw back her head and tinkled with laughter. Stupid cow.

Maggie wondered how she could have even thought for a minute he was a nice guy. She should have trusted her initial impression. Blinded by good sex, that's what she'd been. Ok great, fantastic, *toe tingling sex*, but still. She stopped just behind them.

"Did you enjoy our little town's Christmas get together Amy?" she asked loudly, and they both turned to her.

"Oh yes, it was just lovely thank you," Amy answered, "very charming."

"Charming? That's good. The fireworks were grand enough for you?"

"Sure, they were nice."

"Nice? Well isn't that just lovely. Of course I'm sure it was nothing compared to the kind of events they put on wherever it is you come from, but we do our best. Where was it you said you come from again?"

"She didn't," Jack cut in amused. "Something wrong Maggie?"

"Wrong? No, why?"

"You seem a little upset."

"Do I have any reason to be upset Jack?"

"I don't know Maggie, do you?"

Amy looked back and forth between Maggie and Jack. The two of them were staring at each other and the intensity of their gaze was such that she felt if she were to wave a hand between them it would most likely burst into flames. She coughed, choking on the atmosphere and tension that was thick in the air.

"Am I missing something?" she asked, when she was able to breathe again.

Maggie finally broke off from Jack's gaze. She had to, if she didn't she feared she would do something to make herself look foolish, like throw herself into his arms.

"No," she said, turning her head to Amy. "You're missing nothing. You're welcome to him." Then she whirled on a heel and stalked off quickly towards where her mother, father and daughter were waiting under a lamp post, watching her curiously.

"You ok love?" Dot asked as she caught up to them.

"Just fine thank you. Come on, let's get home."

As they walked back to the car she was grateful it was dark enough so that the others couldn't see the tears that welled up in the corner of her eyes and finally, like a burst dam, made their way down her cheeks and nose. She wiped them quickly with one arm and sniffed.

Then she felt a small hand worm its way into hers, the fingers threading through her own. She squeezed her daughters hand and was rewarded with a squeeze back.

Ah bugger Jack; she had everything she needed to make her happy right here.

Chapter sixteen

Maggie barely had time to spare Jack a thought over the next week. She was so busy in her shop with the lead up to Christmas. From the moment she opened the door at nine until the moment she shut it again at six, a steady stream of cars turned into the driveway with people wanting to buy her soaps for loved ones, friends and in some cases, employee Christmas gifts. There were two nights she had to stay up past 2am making more soaps as she had run out of some types.

One afternoon she bribed her mother, with the promise of a cooked dinner and a glass of whiskey, to sit behind the counter and man the shop. Maggie picked Willow up from school an hour early and they spent the afternoon at the lake together. Even though the water still had an edge to it they had a blast swimming and taking turns diving to the bottom to fetch more lake weed.

One night, using Ray as their getaway driver, she let Willow stay up late and they made a night time raid of the town's only supply of mistletoe. It grew on a tree that was located on the sweeping lawns of the town's museum/library. It was difficult to harvest and Maggie only bothered at Christmas time. She and Willow dressed head to foot in black, which probably wasn't totally necessary but which made them feel like

Ninjas. They made a game out of it, ducking behind hedges and trees and crawling army style along the grass, until Ray, fed up with being stuck in the car and missing out on the fun, tooted the horn loudly and yelled at them to "get a bloody move on!" Her mistletoe soap was popular at Christmas as it calmed hysteria, tension headaches, nervous attacks and anxiety, all common ailments of the holiday season.

On the Friday Willow finally finished school for the year and they went to Nick's parent's house for a BBQ to celebrate. Other kids from school were there with their parents, and a couple of the single dads flirted with Maggie as they always did at parent evenings and galas and such. But even though she had made a promise to herself to be more receptive to that kind of thing and to not say no so easily, she just couldn't summon any interest in any of them.

Saturday night the four of them, Maggie, Dot, Ray and Willow, spent the night decorating the house. Dot had already put some decorations up earlier in December. Others stayed out all year round, like the sticker of a snowman in the front window that was faded from sun exposure and peeling back at one corner, and the small ornamental light in the corner that had a plastic candy cane inside. When you shook it upside down it glowed red, green and blue and glitter swirled up like a snowstorm and Willow had been utterly transfixed with it when she was a baby. Ray dug the boxes of decorations out from the cupboard under the stairs and they opened them up and spent time untangling fairy lights and tinsel and restringing cotton on the end of sparkly baubles. Ray had bought a tree off a guy on the corner somewhere, and he and Maggie dragged it inside, leaving a trail of pine needles in their wake. They wedged it into a bucket with bricks to help it stand and displayed it proudly in the corner of the lounge. They had to trim the tip of the top off as it was so tall it scraped the roof.

"It's a beauty," Dot declared.

"Smell that smell?" Ray breathed deep, "that's the true smell of Christmas. That and sweet sherry of course," he added draining the small glass Dot had poured him. Luckily they all preferred a mismatched style of decorating, and so they randomly took turns draping the lengths of silver, gold, red, green and blue tinsel around the branches, and hanging a collection of homemade and shop bought decorations on the tips.

"Oh I remember when you bought this home," Maggie said, her eyes misting over as she clutched a cardboard Santa that Willow had painted in her last year of Kindergarten.

"Yikes, not very good at painting inside the lines, was I?"

"I don't care, it's perfect to me. Oh and look at this one you made when I took you to baby art classes! It has your little hand print in paint on the glass." She sniffed.

"Are you going to cry over every decoration mum? Cause if so this could take awhile."

"Cheeky. Only the sentimental ones."

When they had finished, a few hours and a few more sherry's later, the house looked like Santa's grotto. With the main lights off and only the lights on the tree and the candy cane light glowing the room was warm and cosy and magical. Tinsel glittered and the soft sound of old carols played softly on the stereo.

It was a truly wonderful night.

But even though she was busy and *technically* didn't have the time to spare Jack a thought, when she did finally tumble into her bed, she would lie awake, staring at the shadows on her ceiling, and she remembered how it had felt to be with him.

Chapter seventeen

Meanwhile, across town, Amy was regretting her decision to leave her job as a beauty therapist for a career change as Receptionist/Office manager/Vet assistant at the Veterinary clinic. Admittedly, when she'd gone for the interview she had taken one look at him and decided then and there that if she was offered the job she would take it, no question. But working for him was like paradise gone wrong. He was moody and sullen at the best of times, and apart from gruffly asking her every now and then whether he'd had any messages he barely spoke to her. Her woman's intuition told her it had something to do with Maggie, the lady who'd stormed off in a strop the night of the carols.

Jack, meanwhile, lay awake for much the same reasons as Maggie. That damn woman, he fumed, was annoying, frustrating and bewildering with her mood swings and childish behaviour, but by god she intrigued him.

He yearned for her about as much as he was determined to stay away from her.

Chapter eighteen

In hindsight Maggie should have known that bad news would shortly be forthcoming.

Certainly she knew something was up. From the moment she got out of bed and tripped on the corner of the rug, banging her shin on the dresser and watching in dismay as a large yellow bruise surfaced, to the moment she limped out to the kitchen and saw that someone had left bacon frying and small flames were licking at the air from where the hot oil had caught, she knew that something wicked was in the air.

"Dammit," she swore, flicking the switch at the wall to turn the oven off. She quickly grabbed a tea towel and ran it under the tap, then wringing most of the water out she threw it over the pan. Then she grabbed another tea towel and repeated the process. Once she was sure the flames were contained she wrapped some of the damp towel around the handle and carefully carried the whole thing out the back door, throwing it down onto the grass well away from the house.

She went to unravel the hose and found it all twisted with knots upon knots, even though she knew for a fact that the previous evening after she had watered the vegetable beds she had wound it up tidily and in a neat coil.

Her dad popped his head out the back door.

"Ah," he said, "Oops."

"Oops? That's all you've got to say for yourself? You could have burnt the house down," she fumed.

"Nonsense. No harm done. I would have been back long before that happened."

"It was only about ten seconds away from happening. Where were you?"

"I had to make an unplanned bathroom stop."

"Christ dad, next time take the bloody pan off the heat. Seriously, this could have been really bad." She finally got the hose to behave and turned it on, aiming the water at the pan.

Ray realised how upset she was. "Sorry love," he said. "I promise it won't happen again."

"It better not. I'm not having Willow exposed to any danger. You start pulling crap like this and we'll either move out or put you in a home, you got it?"

"Got it." He saluted then disappeared back inside the house. Ten seconds later he re-emerged.

"Er, sweetheart, let's just keep this between us, aye?" he fidgeted his feet nervously. "No need to tell your mother."

Dot was famously scared of dying in a house fire. It was the one thing that terrified her, ever since she was a little girl and had been woken one night by screams as her neighbour's house burnt to the ground. Luckily, the people had all escaped, but the family dog wasn't so lucky. Dot had loved that little dog and she mourned him greatly. A fox terrier named Dash; he used to meet her at the gate when she got out from school and walk home with her. She considered him one of her best friends. Ever since his grisly and untimely death she had been extremely fire safety conscious. The wiring in the old house was checked every ten years and every room in the house had been fitted with a smoke alarm. Ray knew Dot would most likely kill him, or at the very worst seriously maim, if she found out what he had done.

Maggie gave him her most serious glare. "We'll see. Depends on whether you pull any more stupid stunts like this." Then something occurred to her and she frowned. "I wonder why the smoke alarm didn't go off. We checked them all last daylight savings and the batteries were fine."

"Ah," Ray winced, "About that…"

"What have you done?"

"I *may* have pulled the batteries out last time your mother went bush and the boys came round for poker."

"Oh for god's sakes dad, why would you do that?"

"You and Willow were asleep," he protested, "and some of the guys were smoking cigars. I didn't want the alarm to go off and wake you."

Maggie rubbed her temples warily and wondered if it were too late to crawl back under the covers and start this day again in another hour or so.

"Just fix them dad," she said. "Replace all the batteries and make sure they work and I *might* not tell mum what you've been up to."

"Righto. Thanks love." He disappeared back inside the house again. She peeled the tea towels off the pan and realised they were beyond saving. Reluctant to throw them away she decided they'd be just fine as rags for her father in his shed.

"Ahem."

Her father was once more hovering at the back door.

"What now?"

"Any hopes some of that bacon could be saved?"

"*Oh for the love of...*" She took a deep breath and counted to ten. "No dad. It's completely charcoaled."

"That's a shame." He vanished inside again.

Shaking her head she took a deep breath. "Give me strength," she muttered. She walked over to the fence and draped the towels over it to air dry.

It was then she noticed how still the air was.

Not still like you sometimes get on really hot days when even the breeze can't be bothered dragging itself out from the shady spot it was dwelling in. It wasn't that kind of still.

It was more like the ominous still you get just before a really big storm hits, only today there wasn't a cloud in sight. She licked a finger and held it out just to be sure, but as suspected there wasn't even a hint of a breeze. It unnerved her, and she had a horrible feeling that she was being watched. She shivered and wrapped her arms around herself, suddenly cold.

Back inside her father was standing on a chair and slotting the smoke alarm back into place.

"All present and working again," he said. Then he saw her face. "What's wrong?"

"Nothing," she said, because nothing was wrong exactly, at least nothing that she could pinpoint, but she just couldn't shake the ill feeling that had stolen over her.

Opening her shop, she flitted from job to job, but nothing went right. She swept the floor, making sure she got all of the dust out of the corners that had been dragged in over the previous few days. But just as she had it all gathered in one big pile at the front of her shop, the door flew open with a huge gust and all the dust went scuttling back to where it had come from. When she stepped outside though, the air was just as still as it had been earlier, not even a single leaf was rustling in a tree.

Despite being inundated with customers every other day that week, not a single car turned into their driveway that morning. She walked down to the end of the road, thinking maybe the sign had been vandalised or stolen like it had once before but no, it was hanging where it always hung, not a mark on it.

The letterbox.

She frowned at the letterbox. Maybe there was something bad in the letterbox. She closed her eyes and opened it quickly, like she was ripping a band aid off, and slowly opened one eyelid to peer inside. A pile of envelopes greeted her but flicking through them there was nothing to warrant the ill feeling she had.

Willow.

She closed the shop, calling out to her father who was watching Baywatch in the lounge to tell anyone who came that she would be back in an hour, and she drove to Nick's house. Willow, lying with Nick on the trampoline, was alarmed to see her mother jump out of the car, flushed and worried.

"What's wrong mum?" she asked, jumping down from the trampoline. Her mother gathered her into a tight hug and exhaled the breath she'd been holding the entire drive there.

"Nothing's wrong baby. I just wanted to see my girl."

"I'm almost eleven mum, not stupid. You promised no more secrets remember?"

Her mother smiled. "Right. Sorry. But I'm not lying, nothing *is* wrong. I just really wanted to see you."

Willow studied her mother's face and could see that she was being honest.

"Ok I believe you. It's still a bit weird though, you just turning up like this."

"I know, and I promise not to embarrass you like this too often. Do you want to come home with me for lunch?"

"Nah, Nick's mum is making us a pizza. Can I stay for that?"

"Of course. That's fine. Just stay safe ok, and if you can't be bothered walking home call me and I'll come and get you."

"Are you sure everything's ok? There's nothing's wrong with gran or granddad?"

Maggie bent down to Willow's level and put her hands on her shoulders. She could tell that she'd freaked her daughter out and she wanted to reassure her. "No, they're fine. Everything is fine, I promise."

"Ok." Willow kissed her mum quickly and then climbed back up onto the trampoline. Maggie watched her go, wishing as she often did that she could wrap her daughter in bubble wrap and keep her always by her side. She'd been fighting that urge since her daughter emerged into the world, eyes open and curious right from the first moment.

"I love you," she called to Willow.

"I love you too mum."

Maggie drove home feeling happier with the knowledge that her daughter was safe, but still with the nagging feeling that a storm was brewing.

Nick and Willow watched her drive away.

"Your mum is weird sometimes" Nick said.

Willow sighed. "Tell me about it."

"Guess that's where you get it from then huh?"

"Shut up!" Willow slapped his leg leaving a red hand print.

"Ow that hurt!"

"Serves you right."

Things kind of returned to normal once she was back home, in that customers started to trickle in, her father managed not to start any more fires and enough of a breeze sprung up so that Dot was able to get some washing dry. She had returned from a catch up with friends to find her best frying pan in a blackened patch on the lawn but with no one confessing how it had got there. Both Ray and Maggie had clammed up and were claiming ignorance, but she knew the truth would come out eventually. It always did.

So Maggie had just started to relax and think that whatever had been bothering the world that morning had passed, when she looked out of the door of the shop and saw Geoffrey the policeman standing there watching her, his hat in his hands.

Her heart stopped beating in her chest and a hand flew to her mouth. Her first thought was for Willow, and thankfully Geoffrey could read that on her face because he opened the screen door and stepped inside quickly, his eyes anxious.

"It's ok Maggie," he said, "I'm not here about your daughter."

"Oh thank god," she whispered, her knees giving away so she slumped back against the counter.

"I'm sorry I frightened you like that," he went on, "people always assume the worst when they see me. It's an occupational hazard."

Maggie recovered her voice. "So you're not here with bad news?"

"Well now I didn't say that, or if I did I didn't mean it like that, I get my words muddled sometimes sorry, it's always –"

She cut him off. "Geoffrey, why are you here?"

"Oh right. Is there somewhere we can talk?"

"Something wrong with right here?"

"Somewhere you can sit down I meant, might be better. Are your folks home?"

"Yes, they're both here."

"You might want them with you."

"Geoffrey you're scaring me."

"I'm not meaning too, I'm sorry. Look," he turned and closed the shop door behind him and turned the OPEN sign to CLOSED. "Let's just go inside the house."

Maggie could hardly walk, her ankles kept turning in and her bones felt like they had become disconnected from each other. She led the way into the lounge where Ray was snoring on the couch and poked him. He rolled over with a grunt but didn't wake. Maggie poked him harder and this time he opened his eyes grumpily.

"What?" he complained. "What does a man have to do to get some peace around here?" Then he saw Geoffrey and his expression soured even more. "What are you doing here?" he struggled to sit up. "I haven't been on the bike again, and if anyone says otherwise they're lying."

"Relax," Geoffrey said, "I'm not here about your bike."

Dot had been upstairs changing the sheets on the beds when she heard voices and came down to investigate.

"What's going on?" she asked, coming into the lounge. "Oh hello Geoffrey." She turned to Ray, "have you been out on that blasted bike again?"

"No, I haven't," Ray protested under her glare.

"It's ok Dot," Geoffrey backed him up, "I'm not here about that. Not this time anyway."

"Then what?" Dot looked at Maggie and saw that her daughter's face had turned as pale as the faded curtains behind her. 'Oh my god is Willow ok?"

"She's fine mum."

"Oh thank god," Dot clutched at her chest and sank onto the couch beside Ray. She had in that moment of fear appeared twenty years older and as frail as a baby bird. "Then what is it?"

"I don't know mum, I'm waiting for Geoffrey to hurry up and tell us."

Three expectant faces turned to him and he farted nervously under the pressure. Dot and Maggie pretended out of politeness that they hadn't heard but Ray openly smirked.

Geoffrey cleared his throat. "I'm not sure if you've already heard - you know what this town is like for gossip, spreads like damn wildfire. I swear this one time, everyone knew that Bruce Jameson had assaulted his wife before he'd even laid a finger on her. And there was that time in the middle of the night when you would assume of course that everyone is fast asleep but I swear, it was all over town before I'd even had my breakfast that –"

"*Geoffrey,*"

"What? Oh, sorry." He farted again and coughed to cover it up.

"Earlier in the week a hunter stumbled across a body at the base of an old waterfall," he told them. "We're still waiting on official identification using dental records, but the belongings found with the body suggest it's that of your husband Maggie."

"My husband?" she was confused. It was so long since anyone had used the word in context to her that she was unaccustomed to hearing it.

"You mean Jon?" Ray asked.

"Yes," Geoffrey nodded. "Jon Tanner."

Maggie leant back into the couch, speechless.

"I don't understand," Dot frowned, "you mean he's been in this area the whole time?"

"Oh I wasn't clear, sorry. It was pretty obvious that the body had been there for a long time. Some letters and a newspaper in a bag he had on him date back to December 2007."

Maggie gasped.

"Oh my god," Dot put a hand over her mouth. "That means -"

"What?" Ray asked, looking from face to face quizzically.

"He's been dead this whole time," Maggie finished the sentence for her mother.

"Oh."

"I'm sorry to bring you the sad news Maggie," Geoffrey said. "It's the only part of this job I really dislike."

"No it's ok Geoffrey, thank you for letting us know. So what happens now?"

"We should have the official identification through tomorrow, after that the coroner will release the body to you I guess, as next of kin. I can give you the number of the local funeral home, they're pretty good at pulling together services at the last minute. I assume you want to organise it Maggie," he asked delicately, "if not the state will take care of it."

"Of course we'll organise it," Ray snapped. "He's Willow's father for god sake."

"Dad," Maggie placed a hand on his arm. "He's only doing his job." She turned to Geoffrey, "Yes, of course we'll organise everything."

"Thanks Maggie," he smiled gratefully. "Are there any family I need to notify or will you take care of that?"

Maggie closed her eyes. Her mind was a whirl of thoughts and she was fighting the urge to get up and run from the room to somewhere quiet so she could sort her thoughts out. "No," she finally answered. "I don't think so. His mother died when he was only small and his dad remarried and left town when he was in high school. Last I heard he had moved to Australia for a new life, but that was a long time ago. Leave it with me; I'll see what I can find out."

"Ok, I appreciate that Maggie." Geoffrey put his hat back on his head and pushed it down. "I'll be in touch tomorrow. In the meantime you let me know if there's anything I can do to help."

Maggie nodded but her mind had already started to wander. It felt unreal, like she was having an out of body experience, watching while this happenned to someone else.

Dot walked Geoffrey to the door but just as he stepped over the doorstep to leave Maggie stood and hurried over to him.

"Wait," she called. He turned back.

"Yes?"

She stopped in front of him and bit her lower lip. She wasn't sure how to ask the question she needed to ask.

"Maggie?"

"Was it quick? I mean, can they tell whether he suffered or not?" she choked off a sob with the last words and Dot put a hand out to steady her.

Geoffrey shook his head. "He didn't suffer Maggie."

"But how can you tell? If he's been just, *lying* there for so long?"

Geoffrey looked at Dot who nodded, "If you know something that can ease the worry then say it," she told him.

"From the looks of it he broke his neck pretty bad when he fell. He would have died instantly."

"Oh thank god," Maggie squeezed her eyes shut. Then she opened them again, "That's not what I mean," she said, "I was, you know –"

"We understand," Ray came to join them at the door. He put his arms around his daughter and placed his stubbly cheek against her head. She relaxed into him, wondering when the last time was that she had been hugged like this by her father. He felt and smelt so familiar, like an old jersey you can't bear to part with.

"Mum? Willow's voice startled them all. She had come up on the porch so quietly they hadn't heard her. "Mum what's wrong? Why is Geoffrey here?"

'I'll leave you guys to digest the news," Geoffrey said again, "but please call me if there is anything I can do."

"Thank you," Maggie nodded. She reached an arm out for Willow who curled into her side.

"Mum?"

Maggie took a deep breath. "We need to talk."

Chapter nineteen

Hours later, when Willow was tucked up in bed and asleep, Maggie poured herself a large glass of red wine and wandered barefoot out onto the porch. She sat on the step and took a large gulp, swirling the wine around her mouth as its slightly acidic taste set her taste buds on edge. She swallowed it and let out a breath. The sky was clear and massive, endlessly stretching above her, the Milky Way a playful streak through the centre.

Where to even begin to process what she had learnt the last few hours?

Busy making sure Willow was ok, lying in bed beside her and stroking her hair while doing her best to answer the questions Willow had, she hadn't yet had time to process her own feelings. Listening to her daughter snuffle softly as she gave in to sleep had been heartbreaking. Her daughter might only have vague memories of her father and might have believed all this time that she didn't miss him, but it was an entirely different matter to find out that he had died. The only slightly good thing to come out of any of it had been the realisation that Jon hadn't abandoned Willow after all. That part had never made any sense.

Maggie had no words to describe the relief she felt, knowing that Jon hadn't left his little girl by choice, that he would have been here in her life all these years if he hadn't met the fate he had. It was like years of bitterness and anger had just peeled away like the bitter layers of an onion, leaving only the sweet centre to remain.

She felt carefree and light, like she could dance across the grass and into the sky, tip toe from star to star and be back again by morning.

Did she feel guilt for feeling such relief when the cause of that relief was so tragic? Yes, but only a smidgeon. Because she also felt varying degrees of grief, and sadness for a life cut so short. For a father deprived of his daughter, and a daughter deprived of her father. Therein lay the most heartbreak for Maggie.

As for herself, who knew whether her marriage would have survived all these years? If she was honest, she doubted it. They were young with no idea how to fight fair or how to compromise. They embarked into marriage with only romantic ideals in mind, no inkling of the hard work that would be needed to sustain it. She was sad for Jon, sad that his life ended so horribly and all alone. She had loved him terribly once, had felt him to be everything to her, but that love was long since extinguished.

If he had to have died, at least he had died in the place that he loved, they could be grateful for that.

The service was held three days before Christmas. In the morning the sky was pale grey and a fine drizzle gave the land some much needed nourishment. At noon, as if a switch had been flicked, the sky turned blue and the sun appeared high above them.

Jon hadn't been a particularly religious man so they held the service by the lake, under the shadows of the hills he considered home. Maggie had managed to track down Jon's father, retired and living in a hostel and barely able to walk as the result of a stroke, so he could not attend. He sent a card that Ray read out, it was neither emotional nor overly personal, merely words as if from a friend.

Maggie stood and read a brief eulogy. It was sketchy on details from his early life, as he had always spoken of it as if it were not much to speak of. Instead she embellished the happy years, the way he cried when his daughter entered the world, and how, in the very early years at least, he was there every night to bathe her, read her a story and rock her to sleep. It had been their time, his and Willow's, and no one but them would ever be privy to the loving words he had whispered as he kissed her and nuzzled her little face. Willow might not remember the exact words, but she had a fuzzy recollection of a voice in her ear and lips on her cheek, and she had the closure now of knowing where her father was and why he wasn't with her. And that was the most important thing.

The small group of attendees sang Amazing Grace, and their voices glided over the water and bounced off the hills, as if a choir of one hundred were there and not just a few.

Afterwards, people were invited back to the house for refreshments. Harper and Wade headed back to the house to sort things out there so Maggie, Willow, Dot and Ray could attend a private cremation ceremony for Jon. They watched as the coffin was lowered into the floor and the minister read out the committal words. Maggie shed some tears finally, her first since the news had been delivered. Before the coffin was lowered she stepped up to place a flower on it, and she whispered an apology for all the ill thoughts she had harboured towards him for all these years.

Willow kissed the top of the coffin and placed an envelope amongst the flowers to be cremated with him. It was a letter she had stayed up late the night before to write, and its contents would stay between the two of them for always.

Maggie was proud of her daughter and the way she had handled everything. If she had been in any doubt that her daughter was no longer a child those doubts were long gone.

Outside the crematorium, the four of them huddled into a hug.

"It was a lovely service," Dot said.

"It was," Ray agreed.

"He would have been happy with that."

"He would."

"Thanks guys," Maggie said. "And thanks for all your help. I couldn't have pulled it together last minute without you."

"Of course darling, it's what we're here for."

"You ok kid?" Ray asked Willow, reaching out to ruffle her hair.

"Get off," she ducked. Then when she was out of arms reach she stopped and nodded. "I'm ok. Are you ok mum?"

Maggie smiled at her. "I'm fine sweetheart."

They linked arms and walked back to the car slowly, each processing the last few days. Nothing really had changed, at least not in their day to day lives. It was still just the four of them, their little square family as Ray called them.

But also, everything had changed. They had knowledge now. They knew where he'd gone and why he hadn't come back. And they knew that he would never be coming back. The memories they had of him were all they would ever have, so they needed to polish them up, scrub off the tarnish that had accumulated and display them in a new light. He wasn't a father who abandoned his wife and child; he was the victim of a tragic accident that had taken him away from them.

And that made all the difference in the world.

Chapter twenty

"I'm sorry for your loss."

Maggie froze and closed her eyes. She had been sliding sandwiches from one plate to another in the kitchen when the voice spoke beside her ear and its tones reached in and plucked her heart like the strings on a harp so that it vibrated in her chest. She waited for it to be still again before she opened her eyes and turned, her voice emerging calmly.

"Thank you."

She hadn't realised he was at the service until she'd stood and turned to read her speech, then she'd spied him, his tall hulk in the back row of white deck chairs, his eyes on her and her only. She'd faltered briefly, and the only way she'd got through the speech was to ignore him and pretend he wasn't there.

"How are you going?" he asked.

"I'm fine."

"And Willow? How is she coping?"

"She's ok, she's handling it better than I would have expected. I guess not seeing him in so long means it hasn't affected her as much as it could have. She's sad, but she's coping."

"That's great. I'm glad to hear it." He smiled genuinely when he said it and Maggie pondered on how familiar that smile seemed to her already, and how much she'd missed it lately. It was the kind of smile you'd do anything to see. The sort that if you woke up next to it, it would put you in a brilliant mood for the rest of the day.

"Where's Amy?" she looked behind him in case the pretty young lady was lurking back there.

"Amy? She's at work."

"Work?"

"One of us had to hold down the fort. Not that she'd be any good in an actual emergency; the woman spends more time on the phone to friends than anything else." He sighed. "I know I'm going to have let her go, but 'm a bit chicken when it comes down to actually doing it."

"She works for you?"

"Yes, the new surgery receptionist. The old one retired."

Maggie bit her bottom lip to keep from laughing out loud with relief.

Jack noticed. "Wait, did you think -?"

And Maggie couldn't deny it so she turned and busied herself with the sandwiches instead.

"Well well," he moved beside her to lean against the bench and cross his arms over his chest. "So you thought Amy and I were an item. *That's* why you acted like a mad woman at the carol singing – you were jealous."

"I was not," Maggie protested, but her flushed cheeks said otherwise.

"I guess this means you don't hate me after all."

"I already told you I don't hate you. Hate is a strong word and I prefer not to use it unless absolutely necessary."

"You don't hate anyone?"

She pretended to think. "I'm not overly fond of the tax department taking a huge chunk of my earnings but still, I probably wouldn't say I hate them."

"So you like me."

"You could say that."

"Even," his tone turned serious, "after all the things I said to you. I was way out of line and I want to apologise."

"No, you were spot on. Not with everything, but *most* of what you said." She sighed dramatically. "I *suppose* I owe you a thank you."

He pretended to clutch his chest in shock. "Wait, am I correct in thinking that not only are you admitting that I was right about something, but you're also *thanking* me? Without being prompted?"

"Don't get used to it."

He held up his hands. "Oh I won't, believe me. I'm well aware you could flip and start telling me off again at any moment."

She poked him in the chest indignantly and he laughed, grabbing her hands and holding them hostage.

"Maggie where are those sandwiches? We've run out of sausage rolls and – oh." Dot stopped. "Hello Jack," she said. "Nice of you to come today."

"Hi Dot," Jack pushed off the bench and gave her a kiss on the cheek. "It was the least I could do. I wanted to show my support for you all."

"I'm sure Maggie appreciates it."

"Here are the sandwiches mum," Maggie passed over the plate she'd arranged. "That's the last of them though. After this there's only the egg salad that Arihana brought with her, if anyone wants some of that."

"I'm not serving her salad. Knowing her there's half a cup of curry powder in it. She's never understood that the rest of us don't have a cast iron gut like she does. Honestly, the last time Ray ate some of her egg salad he damn near sh-" she stopped suddenly as she realised where she was and who she was talking to. "Well, I don't suppose we all need to know what happened next. It's bad enough I do."

"No mum, we really don't need to know."

"Actually I'm kind of curious," Jack deadpanned.

"Don't be so gross," Maggie elbowed him.

"Honey, can I have a quick word in the other room please?"

"Sure mum," Maggie wiped her hands on a tea towel and followed her mother out to the bottom of the stairs. "What's up?"

"You know I like Jack, and you know what I think about the two of you together, yes?"

"Yes."

"It's just that *now* might not be the most appropriate time."

"For what?"

"To you know, be seen flirting with each other."

"What are you on about? We're just talking."

"*I* know that, but others might not realise it's as innocent as that. Just with it being the day of your husband's funeral you might want to mingle with some of the other people here."

"I wasn't flirting for gods' sakes. And Jon hasn't been my *husband* in any sense of the word for a very long time."

"Sweetheart, I know that, but the chemistry between you two is pretty obvious, even to your father who's clueless when it comes to such things. People are noticing."

"Since when have you cared what people think?"

"Oh honey you know I don't care. I'm just worried that *you* might care. Or that someone might say something stupid that might upset Willow."

She had Maggie there. Even though she was doing nothing wrong, she could see how it might appear to others. "Ok," she said. "Ok I get it." She smoothed her skirt down over her thighs and tucked a stray strand of hair behind her hair. "Let's just get this over with. I'm sick of the sight of people today. How small minded of people to think I would be so shallow? I'm not looking to jump into bed with anyone, and certainly not Jack Cartwright."

"I should get going," Jack said from the archway behind her. Maggie spun around.

"I'm sorry," she apologised. "I didn't know you were there."

"Don't worry about it. I wasn't eavesdropping, just thought I'd better get back to the surgery and make sure Amy hasn't burnt it to the ground or lost an animal or something stupid like that."

Dot shuddered at the mention of fire.

His tone had switched from earlier in the kitchen; then it had been playful, now it was serious.

"Thanks again for coming." Maggie knew he had heard what she'd said, hence the change in his manner, and she felt awful but unable to backtrack or bring the subject up again with her mother in earshot.

"You're welcome. Obviously I didn't know your husband, but I'm sure he would have been proud of the send off you've given him."

"I'll walk you out," Maggie said, walking through to the lounge towards him, but Jack shook his head dismissively and backed away.

"There's really no need. You have other guests more deserving of your attention." Then he nodded slightly and left, striding across the room through the throng of people without a backwards glance.

Maggie felt an overwhelming urge to run after him, to explain that she'd just been angry when she said that last comment, but she could feel eyes upon her so she straightened her shoulders and turned to the room instead.

"Happy now?" she spoke to no one in particular, and the people nearest averted their eyes.

"Who are you talking to?" Willow came up beside her.

"No one sweetheart. Have you had something to eat?"

"Yep. Arihana keeps trying to get me to try her egg salad, but I remember what happened that time granddad ate it so there's no way I'm going near it."

"Sensible girl."

"Can I go play outside with Nick now?"

234

Maggie looked her daughter up and down. Dot had taken her shopping for something to wear for the funeral, as Willow's wardrobe consisted mostly of torn shorts and t-shirts. Maggie had been surprised with the result when Willow emerged downstairs that morning.

"Ok what gives?" she'd asked Dot quietly.

"What?"

"How much did you have to pay her to get her to wear that?"

Dot looked at her granddaughter proudly. "Not a cent. In fact she chose most of it herself."

Maggie didn't believe her. Willow was wearing black tights, a neat little knee length pleated black skirt and a pretty little black three quarter length sleeve shirt, with ribbons that tied in the back and an embroidered lace collar. On top of that, she was wearing her hair in a long tidy plait, and, as far as Maggie could tell, she'd even polished her shoes. It was so far removed from anything her daughter had ever let herself be dressed in that Maggie couldn't accept it was by choice.

"Come on now," she'd said sceptically to Dot, "you must have promised her something."

"No."

But Maggie remained unconvinced. Ah well, the truth will come out later, she had thought. It always does.

"Sure you can go and play," she said, "but change out of those clothes first."

"Oh thank god. I've been feeling like a bloody boarding school freak all day." Willow darted off in the direction of the stairs and Maggie frowned. Definitely something must have been promised in order to get her daughter to wear those clothes. She would get to the bottom of it later.

"Don't swear," she called after her daughter.

Chapter twenty one

As soon as Maggie opened her eyes it hit her; tomorrow was Christmas Eve.

Normally the very thought would send her groaning back under the covers, but not anymore. The ghosts of Christmases past had been banished. There was no need for her to spend the day wallowing under a big black cloud of dark memories.

Yes, Jon had left her and Willow on Christmas Eve. But he'd intended on coming back, that much she was sure of now. And whether or not the marriage would have lasted, he would have been around for his daughter, she was also sure of that.

Humming the song White Christmas she threw back the covers and after a few stretches, she took an unreasonably long shower using her lemon soap to enhance her new zest for life and the holiday season in general. Even though it was Christmas and a certain degree of excitement was inevitable, she felt it was more than just that brewing inside of her. There was something else in the air. She could sense it and occasionally she nearly caught a glimpse of it but when she turned her head quickly it was gone, dancing out of sight. She felt something she hadn't felt in years; girlish glee, and she couldn't wait to see what lay ahead. Not just today or tomorrow, but next week and next month. Everything seemed open and endless, and absolutely anything seemed possible.

It was like the feeling you get when you're a child on Christmas Eve and before you get tucked up in your cosy bed you admire the lights twinkling on the tree and the angel beaming down at you from the top, and you know that the next time you see that tree there's going to be presents stacked underneath it, a lot of them with your name on. Or that goodwill feeling that floods you when you know that you have your family around for you for the foreseeable future; that no one needs to dash off to work or to school. That you're all together and you have day upon day of summer stretching out ahead with nothing but sunshine and plenty of food and the occasional game of backyard cricket. The feeling you get when life seems effortlessly easy and infinitely enchanting.

That was the feeling she had. And she couldn't wait to see her family and feel the warmth that accumulates any time you have people who love each other, all together in the same room.

She left her damp hair loose and threw on a short summery dress. Her legs, she was pleased to notice, were already lightly tanned from the days spent collecting flowers, leaves and bark for her soaps.

She wasn't sure exactly what she was expecting when she walked out in to the kitchen, but it certainly wasn't the silence that greeted her. Puzzled, she checked the clock in case she had woken early. But no, it was a little after eight. Everyone was normally well up by now and the kitchen a hive of activity.

Her mother would normally have been preparing breakfast, or food for Christmas day. Her father should have been parked behind his paper, only his fingers on each side and the top of his head visible. Willow tended to be seated at the table fidgeting, either eating too fast or complaining that the food was taking too long and that she had places to go and things to do.

But the table was empty and the kitchen completely void of cooking sounds and smells.

"That's strange," Maggie said aloud. She went back out to the bottom of the stairs and called up, "Willow? Are you up there?"

She waited but there was no answer and not a sound from above.

"Mum? Dad?" she called.

But again there was no answer. Thinking perhaps they were playing a game she tip toed up the stairs and burst into her daughters room. "Aha!" she said. But the room was empty, and more alarmingly, the bed was made. Now Maggie really started to worry. Her daughter never made her bed without someone nagging her to do it first. She crossed the hall quickly to her parents' room but it was also empty. Her parents slept in matching single beds which were separated by a space of half a metre. They'd been like that for the last ten years, since Dot declared she'd had enough of being kept awake by Ray's constant tossing and turning. This way, they were still in the same room but each slept soundly, and if they needed some private time then they just pushed the beds together. Normally Maggie avoided looking in there because she really didn't need to know when her parents had been, *getting busy*, as Ray termed it.

But everything seemed normal, nothing was out of place. Her mother's bed was neatly made and her father's was a mess of scrunched up sheets and blankets.

She went back downstairs and into the kitchen. She had started to feel a little uneasy, and if this was some kind of game she wanted it over with now. Dishes were drying in the dish rack, so someone had been up and eaten a meal. There was no note on the fridge, where they usually left messages for each other. She picked up the phone and dialled Nick's house. His mother answered.

"Hi Kate," Maggie said, "I'm sorry to call so early."

"Early?" Kate laughed, "It's nearly noon by farming standards."

"Oh of course."

Kate sensed something in Maggie's voice when she didn't join in the laughter.

"Everything ok Maggie?" she asked. "I mean, apart from the obvious. That was a really nice service you gave yesterday by the way. Really nice."

"Thanks Kate. Have you seen Willow? Is she with Nick?"

"No I'm sorry, I haven't seen her today."

"Can you ask Nick if he's heard from her please?"

"Sure, hang on," Kate yelled out for him and then Maggie could hear them talking. She came back on the line after a minute. "No Maggie, sorry. He hasn't seen her since yesterday. Said they made loose plans to catch up later today but nothing concrete. He was going to call her after breakfast. Hang on a sec," her voice got muffled again. "What? No you idiot, she's not there, that's why I asked you if you'd seen her." She spoke into the receiver again, "Sorry Maggie, Nick wanted to know if he could speak to Willow. Honestly that boy, sometimes I worry he's too much like his father, bless his simple soul."

"Thanks Kate. If you see her can you let me know?"

"Of course. I'm sure she's fine."

"Oh I'm sure too. I'd just like to know where she is. Call me overprotective," she joked feebly.

"I understand completely and I'll call you straight away if we see her."

Maggie hung up the phone and walked to the front door. She could see no one up the driveway, not a soul in sight anywhere. She had to fight a horrible feeling that she was left alone in the world.

"Don't be silly," she told herself, "you just spoke to Kate on the phone."

All the same, she went back to her room to get a cardigan. Suddenly the summer's day felt colder. While she was in her room she heard a noise at the back door and with relief she ran out to the kitchen.

"There you are! You guys had me worried for a minute."

"Morning sugar," her dad kissed her on the cheek and threw his newspaper down on the table.

Maggie looked behind him but he was alone.

"You couldn't rustle me up some brekkie could you sweetheart?" he asked, "and a tea if you're making yourself one." He found his glasses on the top of the fridge and sat down at the table, shaking out the paper in front of him. He started to read.

Maggie walked to the bench and flicked the switch to boil the jug. "Mum didn't cook you any?"

"No, they left too early for me. I was still in the land of nod."

Maggie turned, her eyes narrowed. "When *who* left early dad?"

He froze and ignored the question.

"Dad, when *who* left? Where is Willow?"

"Mmm?"

"Dad!" she marched over and smacked the paper out of his hands down onto the table.

"I knew I'd be the one left to suffer," he complained. "That damn woman."

"Where are they?"

"Your mother took Willow up bush this morning."

"You're kidding me."

"Nope."

"She took my baby girl to her stupid cave?" Maggie was furious. "Just the two of them or have the others gone as well?"

"They've all gone."

"This is too much, she's gone *too* far this time! How dare she take Willow without talking to me about it? And right before Christmas as well?"

"Whoa settle down. It's just for one night, and she had her reasons. They'll be back tomorrow before you know it."

"I should call the cops on her and have her charged with kidnapping."

"Who, Geoffrey? What's he going to do, fart on her?" Ray sniggered.

"It's not funny dad. She can't just take my daughter away without discussing it with me first."

"Relax, she'll -"

"Don't tell me to relax!"

"Well don't scream at me then!"

'I'm not screaming. Trust me, when she gets home, *then* you're going to hear some screaming."

"Don't you think you're overreacting a little bit?"

"I'm not overreacting, she's *my* daughter."

"She'll be fine."

"How do you know that?"

"Because your mother would lay down her life to protect that kid, and you know it."

That shut Maggie up. He was right. Her mother loved Willow as much as she did and would never do anything to harm her. Still, she should never have taken her away without talking to Maggie about it first. Would she have given her permission? No, probably not. Which was the reason, she suspected, for the cloak and dagger departure under the cover of dawn. But why had she chosen to go so close to Christmas? This was a time for families to be together, not spread all over the countryside. She felt some of her earlier excitement desert her.

"I can't believe this," she said quieter, her anger subsiding. The jug whistled cheerfully to announce it had finished its job and she reached idly to flick it off, forgetting it did that all on its own. Her father watched her anxiously, unsure as to whether breakfast was still a possibility.

"She didn't mean to upset you Maggie, that's the last thing she'd want to do, especially at Christmas."

"But that's the whole point dad; I wanted my family around me. For the first time in a long time I'm enjoying this time of the year and I'm excited about what's to come. I feel like she's robbed me of that."

"She'll be back before you know it. This is just something that means a lot to your mother. She took *you* there once too, remember?"

"Oh my god," Maggie sat down at the table. "I haven't thought about that night in the longest time." She must have been about Willow's age or a bit younger when her mother had taken her. She remembered Dot whispering to her at breakfast to pack a bag with some clothes; that they were going somewhere special and it was a secret. She'd been so excited. Back in those days her mother often took off with her friends for the night, and now Maggie was finally going to see where she went. She had packed a bag and then waited with nervous anticipation until Ray finally left the house and her mother announced it was time.

Dot made a quick phone call and shortly afterwards Lois, Hazel and Arihana pulled up. While they waited Dot grabbed some steaks from the freezer and some liquor from the cabinet. Lois had owned an open top convertible back then and on any fine day she could be seen around town with the top down. She believed the wind was there to be felt, and what was the point in owning a convertible if you were going to drive with the top closed?

"May as well buy a regular car," she said to anyone who mentioned it.

"Aren't you afraid your hair will get ruined?" one lady outside the supermarket had asked, her hand patting her own perfectly coiffured hair. Then she eyed Lois's long, loose and wild curls and sniffed.

"Ruined? What – you think the wind is just going to blow my hair right off my head?" Lois had thrown her head back and laughed. "Until you've felt the wind through your tresses, my dear, you haven't lived." And then she'd driven off with a roar.

The day Maggie got to ride in the car she'd understood exactly what Lois was talking about. Sitting in the back seat, sandwiched between the bulks of her mother and Hazel, she'd closed her eyes and heard the wind whistling past her ears and she'd imagined herself in all sorts of places. On cliff tops, a yacht in the middle of the ocean and on a rollercoaster, something she'd seen on TV but never experienced. Feeling the wind tug at her hair and drag it out in one long streak behind her she pretended she was on one of those, hurtling down from a great height.

"Weeeeeeeeee," she'd squealed, and the others had laughed.

She wasn't so fussed with the walk to the cave though. It felt like forever but was probably only an hour or so. Just when she was ready to sit down and say that she couldn't walk another step her mother had declared,

"We're here."

And Maggie had looked around, confused. This was it? All she could see were trees and thick undergrowth. No cave.

"Where is it?"

"You can't see it?" Arihana had smiled, "My dear, open your eyes and let them adjust to the colours of the forest."

Maggie had rolled her eyes but did what she was told, looking around and studying her surroundings. Then she saw it. What had looked at first glance like nothing but a big mossy boulder, didn't actually quite touch the ground. She could see it had a little overhang, and when she pushed aside a bush and made her way around it she gasped. There, just around the corner, invisible unless you were right in front of it, was the entrance to the cave.

"Wow."

"Impressive, isn't it."

"Can I go in?"

"Sure, just let me go first in case a bear has decided to make it home."

"Don't be lame mum. We don't have bears here in New Zealand."

"Are you sure about that?"

And even though Maggie was sure, her mother's twinkling eyes and the taste of the forest on her tongue made her think anything was possible up here.

Thankfully the cave was empty of wildlife, bar the odd scuttling lizard. Inside, Maggie got another surprise. She'd been expecting, well she wasn't sure *exactly* what she'd been expecting, but it certainly wasn't what she saw.

The stone floor was dry and flat and the cave, she estimated, was around five metres square. But it wasn't the cave itself that was so surprising, it was its contents. A stack of folded bedding and thin mattresses were piled up against the wall furthest from her. In one corner at the back a gramophone sat on a small wooden cabinet. Beside it was a basket of records, and thrown over the whole lot was a large plastic cover. Some deck chairs were folded up neatly and stood against the side of the cave, and beside them was another small cabinet, containing what she later discovered to be shelves of non perishable food, beside a small gas two ring cooker.

"Whoa," she said, trying to take it all in. "How did you guys get all this stuff up here."

Hazel had shrugged. "Over the years we've bought things up as we can."

"You guys carried that thing all the way up here?" Maggie pointed at the gramophone. "Looks like it weighs a ton."

"Oh no, for the heavier things we enlisted the help of some willing and capable men," Hazel grinned wickedly at the others. "We swore them to absolute secrecy of course."

"Right let's get this place sorted out," Arihana had said briskly while rubbing her hands together, and with the four of them working they got the place looking cosy in no time. Beds set up, gramophone uncovered, gas cooker at the ready and a small fire set up in the entrance ready to be struck with a match later when the temperature dropped.

"Won't that smoke us out?" Maggie asked.

"No, one of the neatest things about this cave is its natural design. Look," Arihana gestured Maggie over towards the entrance, "up there," she pointed.

Maggie looked up and saw fissures in the rock through which she could see tiny glimpses of far off sunlight.

"What is it?"

"A natural chimney in the rock. All the smoke gets sucked up there and released out through the hills further up. Stops us from getting smoked out, and prevents people from following the smoke to our cave."

The next day, when a tired but happy Maggie and Dot returned home, Ray tried to quiz her on what had taken place up in the cave where he wasn't allowed. But Maggie had taken an oath and wouldn't tell him anything. She refused to tell him about the singing and dancing to the old records, or the feast they'd cooked up of steaks and baked beans, with bread to soak up the sauce and cans of creamed rice to finish the meal off. She didn't tell him how the ladies had drunk wine with their meal and whiskey as a chaser, and they gave Maggie bubbly lemonade in a wine glass to drink which she pretended was wine too. Or that as well as the singing there had been plenty of talking, more talking in fact, than she'd ever heard in one place ever. A lot of it had gone over her head. The women talked about some things that were a mystery to her. They complained about their husbands a fair bit, but having lived with her father Maggie felt that was justifiable. She didn't tell him that she'd been allowed to stay up until two in the morning, when they all finally climbed onto the little beds, and how she'd nestled in beside her mother and looked up out the cave entrance at the stars twinkling through the trees. And she'd lain there and listened to the gentle sound of Hazel snoring, and the soft timbre of her mother's voice as she recited to her the story of Peter Pan off by heart. Maggie was entranced because in the back reaches of the cave, little pin pricks of lights sat listening to the story as well, and what else could they be but fairies? Of course in later years she realised they were probably glow worms, but back then it had felt as if Tinkerbell and the others were right there with her. It had been the most wonderful night of her life, and how special she had felt that her mother and the others had chosen to share their special place with her.

That feeling had stayed with her for a long, long time. Right through her teenage years and on into early womanhood. It was a special connection she had with her mother.

Now, sitting at the table, she tried to remember when she had stopped thinking about it. When had the special feeling worn off? For the life of her she couldn't remember. Somewhere along the way other things had taken up space in her memories and in her heart and she had lost it.

"I remember," she said to her father. "I remember it was wonderful and magical and I loved it."

He smiled at her fondly. "There you go. Don't you want Willow to have the same experience?"

Maggie nodded. Willow would love it.

"Your mother just figured that after everything she's been through this week with her father, she deserved a little getaway."

"That was a nice idea."

"So you're not angry anymore?"

She shook her head. "No. I still wish she'd talked about it with me first though. I'll tell her off when she gets back."

"I'm sure she'll be expecting it."

Maggie stood up again to finish making the forgotten cups of tea.

"So we're good?" her father asked.

"We're fine dad."

"Grand. Any chance of that breakfast then?"

Maggie reached up to the top of the fridge and grabbed the box of Weet-Bix that was sitting there. Then she opened the fridge and got the milk off the inside of the door. She plonked both down in front of him. He watched, puzzled, as she went to a cupboard and picked out a bowl. She put that in front of him too.

"There you go," she announced.

"What's this?"

"Breakfast dad. It's not healthy to have a fried breakfast every day, and if I know you, which I do, you'll overindulge come Christmas Day and spend the next week feeling sorry for yourself."

"So?"

"So why don't you eat light for a couple of days in preparation."

"But Weet-bix? It's hardly a meal is it."

"If it's alright for the All Blacks dad, then it's alright for you."

She kissed him on the head and left the kitchen. She had something she needed to do.

Chapter twenty two

She realised as she was driving into town that she had absolutely no idea where Jack lived. How could she have not found that out? Actually, when she thought about it, there was a lot she didn't know about him. She had been so busy telling him to butt out of *her* life she hadn't bothered to find out anything about *his*. She drove by the vet clinic, not sure if it would be open right before Christmas, but she was in luck. The sign was out front and his truck was in the car park. She parked beside it and then looked at herself in the rear-view mirror. Her eyes were bright and shiny with nervous anticipation.

Was she really going to do this?

Yes, she told herself firmly. She was not going to talk herself into chickening out. Get in, get out and get it done before she could think about it too much. She got out and locked her car and walked quickly up the ramp that led into the surgery. After the way she had talked to her at the carol night Maggie was dreading seeing Amy, but the young lady was nowhere about. There was no sign of anyone in fact, but a bell was sitting on the counter next to a note informing her to ring for service. Maggie gave it a quick shake, alarmed at how loud it sounded in this tiny room. Then she waited a few minutes, pretending to read posters on the wall and the backs of cans of dog food off the shelves, anything to hide how nervous she was feeling. Just as her confidence deserted her and she made the decision to flee, a foot already over the threshold, the door behind the counter rolled open and Jack poked his head through.

"I'll be with you in just a minute," he said. Then he saw who it was. "Oh, it's just you." He straightened up and came through the door, peeling off a pair of latex gloves. Maggie could see that he had a fresh red scratch bleeding on the back of one hand.

"Hi, yes it's just me. I can come back later if you're busy?"

"I'm always busy, but even more so since that dim witted receptionist decided the job wasn't for her and quit right on Christmas. Still, saved me the hassles of firing her I suppose."

"You don't close up over the holiday period?"

He gave her a look like she was dim-witted. "No. Rather inconveniently animals don't stop getting sick just because it's Christmas."

Maggie laughed, embarrassed by her silly question. "Of course. Sorry."

"Not that it's not nice to see you Maggie, because it always is, but was there something you were after? Only I'm a bit busy having a minor disagreement with a cat who won't sit still long enough for me to shave his leg and give him a shot."

"It wasn't anything important, nothing that can't wait until later."

"Are you sure?"

"Of course. You go take care of that cat and we'll catch up another time."

"Ok." But he made no move to go, just stood there and watched as she walked out the door, banging one arm against the frame awkwardly when she stumbled under his gaze. She got half way down the ramp before she stopped and did a little frustrated jig and screamed soundlessly. Then she took a deep breath, gave herself a mental kick up the ass and turned around to march back inside. He was standing in the doorway watching her, an amused smile on his face.

She realised he had seen her little performance.

"Are you feeling ok Maggie?"

She raised her chin and stared him straight in the eyes. "Never better," she said. "Following me again?"

"I know you like to think I'm your own personal stalker but no, I was going to grab the sign and lock the doors. I have so much to catch up with out back I could do without more interruptions."

She frowned. "But what if someone has an emergency?"

"Then they can call my cellphone. The number is plastered on the door and the side of my truck for all to see."

"Oh. That's ok then."

He leant against the doorframe and crossed his arms casually over his chest. "Did you forget something?"

"Forget something?"

"Only you were leaving and then you seemed to have some kind of fit, and now you're still standing here."

"It wasn't a fit, funny guy, I was merely expressing some emotion."

"Well I hope I wasn't the cause of it. Looked painful."

She put her hands on her hips and glared at him. "Shut up."

"Make me."

"Oh my god, you're so annoying!"

"So you keep telling me."

"I'm leaving now."

"You have a good day."

She walked two steps then whirled back.

"What is it about you? No one else annoys me like you do."

He shrugged. "My special talent I guess. They do say everyone has one of some sort."

"It's not talent to annoy someone. Any five year old child can do it. Obviously somewhere along the way you forgot to grow up."

"Where's the fun in growing up? I much prefer a child's outlook on life, don't you?"

"We all have to grow up at some stage."

"To a degree," he conceded. "But how much is entirely up to you. The world would be a much better place to live in if we all maintained some of the imagination we enjoyed as children."

It was such a wise and beautiful thing to say, and he was right, but Maggie didn't tell him that. What was it about him? Why did it only take one look from him, one look where it seemed he saw right into her soul and knew everything about her? And one smile that told her he liked what he saw? A look, a smile and she wanted to fling herself at him and never let go. She felt the desire to be as close to him as humanly possible, not just in a physical sense, although that urge was strong. But in every sense. She wanted to know everything there was to know about him. She wanted to see his smile aimed at her every single day. She wanted to sit on his lap and feel his arms around her, to nestle her head in the crook of his neck and inhale that delicious heady scent that was purely his.

When exactly it had happened she wasn't sure, but somehow he had gone from being someone she couldn't stand the sight of, to someone she never wanted to be out of sight of, ever again.

"Maggie?"

She shook herself out of her reverie. "Hmm?"

"You ok? You seemed lost in your own little world there."

"I'm fine."

And she could swear that he had read her thoughts, as she saw the same longing in his eyes reflected back at her. Neither of them could break the stare and for a moment Maggie felt sure he was about to step forward and kiss her, and she opened her mouth slightly in preparation. But then a loud beep broke the spell and they both stepped backwards.

A car had driven past and tooted at them. They both lifted an arm half-heartedly and waved in the general direction the sound had come from, although neither of them turned to see who it was.

"Right," Jack ran a hand through his hair as if waking from a dream."I'd better get back in there or I'll have a mutiny on my hands."

"Ok," Maggie nodded. But she so badly didn't want to leave him. Then she had a thought. "Do you need some help?"

"Don't you have a shop you need to run?"

She pulled a face. "No, I took the sign down yesterday as I'd planned on spending the day with Willow. My bloody mother scuttled that idea."

"Dare I ask?"

"I wouldn't if I were you."

"Sounds intriguing." He ran his hands through his hair again. "Um, sure, some help would be great, but only if there's nowhere else you need to be?"

"Nope, I'm all yours," she said, and then blushed when she realised what she'd said.

"I like the sound of that."

She blushed even deeper. "Shut up."

"I'm still waiting for you to make me."

"Do you want my help or not?"

"I do."

"Then stop making me blush."

"You do that all by yourself." He stepped to the side and held open the door. "After you."

She stepped past him, acutely aware of the close proximity of their bodies. As she watched him lock the door she remembered how much closer they had been, and the memory of how incredible it had felt made her bite her lower lip hard to suppress her longing. It was either that or lunge and bite him, but it sounded like he'd had enough of that from his patients. She grinned at the thought.

"That's a slightly evil grin. Should I be worried?"

"Not at all," she said innocently, but she wondered what he'd say if he knew the true direction her thoughts had taken.

"Follow me." He led her behind the counter and through the door from where he'd emerged earlier. She admired his body as she followed him down the corridor, her eyes running along his wide shoulders, down the contours of his arms and across to his back, broad at the top but narrower at the waist. A memory of her legs wrapped around that waist flashed across her mind and she stumbled slightly before catching her balance.

"You ok?" he asked, turning when he heard her hand slap against the wall to steady herself.

"Fine, just tripped on the rug."

"There is no rug, just lino."

"Then obviously I tripped on the lino."

"You tripped on the smooth, flat lino?"

"What are you - the tripping police?"

"You're acting weird. Something on your mind?"

"If you only knew."

"Sorry?"

"Nothing. Are we going to do some work or not?"

"Calm down stroppy," he held his hands in front of them palms facing out as if she were a wild horse in need of soothing. "What is it about you Maggie Tanner?"

She sighed exaggeratedly, "We've been here, done this" she said. "And you came up with no answer then either."

"One day I will figure you out. Mark my words."

"We'll see."

They heard a high pitched howl and then a fierce spitting from a room just ahead. Maggie gulped. "That's the culprit?" she gestured towards his injured hand.

"That's him."

"You sure he's just a cat and not actually a wild animal?"

"Oh he's definitely your typical, run of the mill, domesticated tabby. He's just not a very happy one right now. In fact, he's pretty pissed off."

"And you expect me to hold him?"

"You volunteered."

"Is it too late to back out?"

"Oh, it's much too late for that," he said, "there's no going back now." And again she felt there was a second meaning behind his words. It turned out Maggie had a knack for soothing distressed animals. When she stepped into the room behind Jack, hesitant and ready to flee at the first hint of a massacre, the cat leapt off the table and into her arms. She screamed, thinking he was attacking but instead he'd burrowed into her arms and shivered in fear, looking up at her through terrified eyes.

'Shush now baby," she comforted him. "You're ok now, I'm here to protect you from the big nasty man."

"Well I'll be," Jack marvelled. "You've tamed the poor guy. Is no man immune to your charms?"

Maggie smiled smugly and rubbed the cat behind the ears while he purred. "What's his name?"

"Bruno."

She scrunched up a nose. "I see his owner shares your appalling talent for pet naming."

"Hey," he flicked her with one of the latex gloves he was in the process of pulling onto his hands. "I told you Rufus wasn't my choice. Ok, hold him steady on the table and be wary of his teeth."

She did as told but he needn't have worried. Bruno was putty in her hands, and she cooed and told him what a handsome little fella he was while Jack shaved a small section of fur off his paw and gave him the necessary injection. He didn't even flinch when the needle went in.

"What's he in for?" she asked.

"Same thing he's in for every month – an infection from fighting. Bruno here thinks he owns half the town and spends his nights defending his territory. I can't tell you how many claws I've pulled out of his head in the short time I've been here."

Maggie bent down until she was level with Bruno's eyes. "Now listen you," she said sternly, "I want you to stop all this nonsense. Fighting is for bullies, and you are much too cute to be a bully."

Bruno looked suitably shamefaced while Jack snorted. She elbowed him.

"Well?" he protested. "How can you say he's cute? Look at the ugly mug on him."

They both looked at the downcast Bruno. Both ears were missing their tips and he had a large pink scar running across the top of one eye. A fresh nick out of his nose from the latest brawl completed the look.

"I think he's adorable," Maggie declared, kissing Bruno on the head. The cat looked at Jack with what could only be described as triumph.

"Lucky bastard."

"Now now," she tutted, "jealousy doesn't suit you."

Over the next few hours Maggie helped Jack tend to a Labrador with an infected tooth, a parrot with flu, a spaniel with a fractured toe and a cat with a hairball issue. The last patient of the day was a poodle who needed her claws clipped.

"*This* is an emergency?"

Jack sighed. "No, but her owner is apparently one of my biggest donators so," he switched to a baby sing song voice, "if Pookie here needs her nails to look their best for the family Christmas photos, then that's what Pookie wookie will get."

Maggie laughed. She watched as he worked and she felt tenderness towards him. Seeing him like this in his place of work, tending to these animals with care and affection, showed her more than ever that she had been wrong in her initial judgment of him. She might find him intensely annoying at times, but he was also decent and he was kind.

"Right," he finished off the last paw and let it gently back down onto the table. "We're done." He smiled warmly at Maggie, "thank you for all your help today."

"Hey I pretty much just stood around feeling useless, I don't think I was much help at all."

"That's true, you weren't."

"You're not supposed to agree with me!"

"You didn't let me finish. I was going to say that you might not have been much help, but your company was very welcome."

"That's ok then. I forgive you."

"Phew. I don't think I could have slept tonight otherwise."

She remembered how he had looked, lounging in her bed and her breath caught in the back of her throat. She wanted him. She wanted him right then and there, and whenever and wherever she could get him. Christ, she thought, I'm turning into bloody sex obsessed Harper. But she knew that it wasn't just sex she was after, it was Jack.

264

"Thank you, again, for today," he said quietly. "It was nice to spend some time together."

"I enjoyed it."

He checked his watch. "I'd better get Pookie back to her owner before she sends out a search party."

"You deliver the animal home as well? My my, Mr Cartwright, that's quite some service you offer."

He grinned, "Damn straight. No one has ever had cause to complain about my service I assure you."

She groaned. "You just don't stop."

His face was the picture of innocence. "What?"

"Are you doing anything afterwards?"

"Mrs McNeal has asked me to stay for dinner. I think she's trying to set me up with her daughter."

Maggie searched her memory. "Vicky McNeal?" she asked as a connection was made.

He winced. "That's the one."

Maggie suppressed a grin. Vicky McNeal was nice enough, and her cats thought so too, all twenty of them. She wore long skirts and socks with sandals, and the last time a hairdresser had been near her hair she had been wearing a diaper. It was brown and thick and curled past her bottom, and when she sat she had to push it to one side so she didn't sit on it. She campaigned furiously at council meetings on behalf of the ducks at the lakefront and their rights to swim undisturbed by boats, water-skiers and even swimmers. She behaved eccentrically as only those truly coming from wealth can.

"Well do let me know how that works out," Maggie said. "Oh and of course I shall expect an invitation to the wedding." Then she burst into laughter at the horrified expression on Jack's face.

"You evil wench," he said, and for a moment it looked like he might grab her and kiss her as punishment. Or maybe that was simply in her imagination, as he kept his hands firmly at his sides.

"I'd better let you go then," she said, disappointed.

"Thanks again Maggie, for today."

"No problem." She went out through the door he was holding open, then remembered why she had come in the first place and turned back. "Wait, I forgot I came here for a reason."

"Which was?"

"To invite you to our house for Christmas day, that's if you have no other plans?" His face didn't light up with gratitude or pleasure as she'd imagined it would.

"That's a really nice offer Maggie, really. And I'm touched that you'd want me to share the day with you and your family." He took a deep breath and exhaled it slowly, like the next words were hard to say. "But I think that it's probably not the best idea."

"Why not?"

"Well you know, with everything that's happened between us I just think maybe we should both take a step backwards. Let things clear a little, just so there's no confusion."

"Confusion?"

He looked at her like she was being dense on purpose. "Yes, confusion. Between us. And for Willow and your parents and other people in this town."

"I'm inviting you to Christmas dinner, not to make out with me in front of everyone."

"I know that. I just think it'll be better if I don't come. Less, um, what's the word –"

"Confusion?" she offered, hands on her hips and head cocked to one side.

"Yes, confusion. I already said that though didn't I."

"You did."

"You understand where I'm coming from though, right?"

"Oh I understand perfectly," she nodded.

"Good," he smiled with relief. "I'm not always the best at explaining what I mean."

"What I *understand,* is that you are the most frustrating, fickle and aggravating man I have ever had the misfortune to meet."

"Fickle?"

"Yes, *fickle*. You know, flighty, indecisive. If you don't know what it means then look it up in a dictionary." In her anger she borrowed a turn of phrase from her daughter.

Now it was his turn for confusion. "Did I miss something?"

"One minute you're all over me and I'm practically tripping over you every time I turn around. Then the next minute, conveniently after you've got me into bed by the way, you're backing off, saying we need to 'take a step backwards'. Am I correct?"

"Now hang on a minute, that's not what –"

"Oh you're a smooth player alright Jack Cartwright. Thrilled by the chase and then bored with the conquest. Yet you don't have the guts to tell me you're no longer interested, oh no, instead you flirt shamelessly with me all day –"

"Hey you were flirting too -"

"*Then* you tell me you don't want to confuse everyone."

"Yes but I just meant after –"

"Well screw you Jack. I should have trusted my first instincts and run a mile when I first saw you."

"You've got it all wrong, Maggie."

"I don't think so. Enjoy Christmas on your own Jack. Unless, that is, you've already got your next conquest all lined up."

"Now that's not fair," he said angrily. "You won't even let me get a word in edgeways so how can I defend or explain –"

"Yoo hoo!" a voice cooed at the door, startling them both as neither of them had heard the door open. It was Vicky McNeal and she stopped when she saw them. "Phew," she said, fanning her face. "Is it hot in here or is it just me?"

"Vicky, welcome," Jack said in a low voice, his eyes never leaving Maggie's face. "I thought I was returning Pookie to your house?"

"Oh you are," Vicky said, laughing nervously. She could tell she had interrupted something. "I was just in town for other business and thought I would pop in and make sure everything had gone ok."

"Everything went fine, it was a routine nail clipping."

'Oh of course, silly me," she laughed again. "Only would it be ok if I caught a ride home with you? The car was making a funny noise so I've left it at the mechanics."

"Of course," Jack said, his eyes finally breaking from Maggie to flash a tight smile in Vicky's direction. "I just need a minute with Maggie."

"No need," Maggie said firmly, wondering whether Vicky's excuse was genuine. Whether it was or wasn't, it didn't concern her anymore. "I was just leaving."

"We need to finish this conversation."

'No I think we've said everything we need to say."

"Come on Maggie, give me a chance to explain what I meant."

"Like I said, no need. I understand perfectly."

"Maggie –"

"Goodbye Jack. Nice to see you again Vicky."

"Oh I'm sorry, do we know each other?"

Maggie didn't even bother to answer. The tingle in her shoulders as she walked away told her Jack was watching her, but she wasn't going to let him see the tears that had sprung up in her eyes. As she climbed into her car she had to squeeze her eyelids tight to stop the tears from falling because she had a horrible suspicion that if she let them start, they might never stop.

Chapter twenty three

Maggie could see that a summer storm was brewing as she drove home, and it matched her mood perfectly. The sky was ominously grey and the air was quiet and still. She thought of Willow and her mother in the cave and hoped it was as weather proof as she remembered. If Willow got sick from exposure to the elements she would be furious with her mother.

Back home, it didn't take long for Ray to feel her wrath. He could tell as soon as she entered the house that something had upset her; the grey cloud hovering above her head was his first clue. Unfortunately, Ray had never been known for his sensitivity with such matters.

"What's got up your nose?" he asked.

"Nothing," she opened cupboard doors and banged pots. He watched her for a few minutes, but as far as he could tell she wasn't actually planning on cooking anything, just banging and clattering to relieve her mood.

"What has he done now?" he sighed.

"Who?"

"You know who, that nice fella you've been seeing, Jack."

She whirled around and he backed away from the fury on her face.

"What are you talking about?" she said. "Jack is not my 'fella', never has been and never will be."

"But didn't you and he -?"

"Think carefully before you finish that sentence dad. Do you really want to go there?"

He shut his mouth. He'd never been good at talking about the romance stuff with Maggie; that was generally Dot's job and he preferred to stay well out of it. But he hated seeing her upset like this and Dot wasn't here, so he felt he ought to say something.

"Do you want me to go and have a word to him?" he asked.

"Of course I don't! What possible good could that do?"

He shrugged. "It just sounds like something fathers do, you know, on the telly."

"Dad, I appreciate your concern, but I'm fine. I don't want to talk about it."

He sniffed, hurt. "I was only trying to help."

She softened. "I know."

"Maybe if you weren't so stroppy all the time you might not be having this problem?"

She stiffened again. "Stroppy? Me?"

He immediately regretted his choice of words.

272

"Well you know, sometimes you can just be a little bit touchy," he said, inching away from her. "It scares men away. Certainly scaring me right now."

"Oh well excuse me, I'm sorry I'm such a horrible person to live with."

"Come now, I didn't say that."

"As good as. Way to kick me when I'm down, really make me feel better about myself." She went back to taking pots out of the cupboard, finding the matching lids and then shoving them back in.

"Maybe it's your hormones love. Fred says when his wife went through the 'change' it was like living with a murderous demon. He slept with one eye open for months until she finally slapped the butcher for cutting her chops the wrong size and her doctor prescribed her some kind of hormonal patches. He reckons she's bearable again."

"For one thing, I'm far too young to be going through the change, thank you very much. And for another thing, if I had to sleep next to Fred every night I'd probably want to kill him too."

"There's no call for that."

"Just drop it dad, ok. I don't want to talk about it anymore."

"I just want you to be happy love. And if that Jack lad has done something to upset you I want to know about it. Me and the boys will sort him out for you."

That brought a smile to Maggie's face, the image of her father and the other old men fronting up to Jack to defend her. "Thanks dad," she put all the pots back into the cupboard, quieter this time. Then she got up off the floor and kissed him on one lined and stubbly cheek.

"I might go and have a little lay down," she said. "You've got me craving chops now, so I'll cook us some dinner in an hour or so, ok?"

"Ok love."

Maggie had forgotten how much a good cry can sap your energy, so her lay down turned into a nap and when she woke and stretched she was surprised to see the sun had almost set for the night and the walls of her room were bathed in an orange glow from its dying rays. She rolled over and checked the time on the clock beside her bed, just after seven. As tempting as it was to curl back up into a ball and stay there, she knew her father would be getting hungry so she made herself get up. In her ensuite she splashed cold water on her face and was dismayed to see the damage her earlier crying fit had done. She had dark, puffy pillows under her eyes and the whites of her eyes were tinged red.

"Attractive," she remarked dryly.

She expected her father to be asleep in front of the TV but it was switched off and silent in the dark corner, as no lights were on.

"Dad?" she called up the stairs. No answer came.

"Odd," she thought, and going through the kitchen she went out the back door and crossed the yard to the shed. No lights were on in there either and there was no sign of him when she opened the door. Growing slightly alarmed she went back to the house and this time she noticed the piece of paper tacked to the fridge.

'Gone out. Be back later. Leave my dinner in the oven. Love you.'

"Oh dad," she sighed, guessing he had gone to talk to Jack despite what she had said earlier. Then a thought occurred to her. "Oh no, surely he didn't-," she muttered, hurrying back outside to the shed. But indeed he had.

"You stupid, *stupid* man," she stomped her foot crossly.

Her parents shared the one car and as her mother had taken it with her yesterday Ray had taken the farm bike. She stomped back into the house and set about cooking some dinner, anything to take her mind off what her father was doing. She was worried, both about what he might say to Jack, and also that he might end up in a police cell or, worse, in a ditch on the side of the road.

She ate her dinner alone out on the porch, fretting about all her family members; her mother and daughter in a cave in the hills and her father loose on the town on a dangerous bike. She hoped her baby girl was ok, as even though Maggie had been to the cave only once before she knew she had no hope in hell of ever finding her way back there if she ever needed to. She decided she was going to insist her mother buy some kind of hand held radio or cellphone with long ranging service. Dot needed to be able to contact them if, god forbid, something ever went wrong on one of her trips. Maggie already knew her mother would be heavily resistant to the idea, but too bad. Maybe she'd go into town tomorrow and see if she could find one. If she gave it to Dot as a Christmas present she'd have no choice but to accept it.

In the distance the storm was gathering strength over the hills. Occasionally there was a stark flash of silver streaked across the dark sky and the low rumble of thunder building to a climax. Anticipation fizzed through the air and she could smell that rain wasn't far away.

Closing her eyes, Maggie sent up a silent prayer to whoever was listening to keep her family safe then she went back inside to watch some mindless TV for a few hours while she waited for her father to come home. Sometime later she woke with a start at a loud noise, and it took her a moment to realise it had come from the TV. Placing a hand on her chest to still her racing heart she pushed the button on the remote to switch the TV off. Yawning, she walked to the kitchen to check the time; it was just after midnight.

She made her way upstairs and peered into her father's room but the beds were as empty as they had been that morning. Thunder boomed above the house, sending her sagging against the wall and her heart into a sprint once again.

"Oh dad," she whispered. "Where are you?"

Back downstairs in the kitchen she made herself a cup of coffee and drank it standing up against the sink. With the house lights off she could see the storm had finally landed, rain lashing against the windows. She couldn't shake the ill feeling that was tapping lightly on her shoulders. BOOM! Thunder made her jump again. "That's it," she muttered. Pouring the rest of the coffee down the sink she grabbed her keys off the hook and ventured out onto the porch but the driving rain sent her scurrying back inside. In the laundry she found some boots her mother wore while gardening and she pulled them on. The only jacket in sight was Willow's hated strawberry one and seeing it made Maggie long desperately for her daughter, but she couldn't worry about her now. She would just have to trust that her mother was looking after her. Maggie needed to find her father. Wearing the jacket she made her way out into the storm again, the boots and jacket little protection against the almost horizontal sheets of water that came sideways at her. In the car she turned the heater on full and headed off carefully down the driveway as visibility was limited to only a metre or so in front of the car, even with the headlights on full.

Maggie drove the route to and from town four times; there and back, there and back. Each time she drove slower and on the last trip she kept the window wound down so she could call her father's name. Where the sides of the road dropped off into deep ditches she stopped the car, flicking the hazard lights on, and got out, using the torch she always kept in the glove box for emergencies to scan the ground for any sight of him or his bike. But she saw nothing.

Arriving back home the fourth time in tears she finally admitted to herself that she needed help. It was one thirty in the morning and it seemed the rest of the world was tucked up in bed to ride out the storm. But she couldn't rest until she had found her father. She hadn't wanted to alarm anyone but now she had no choice, so one by one she called and roused his friends from their beds. None of them had seen him and all she succeeded in doing was worrying them as much as she was worried.

"What can we do?" they all asked. Trying to hide the fear in her voice she told them there was nothing they could do and that she was already doing everything that could be done.

"I'm sure he's just had a few drinks and is sleeping it off somewhere," she assured them. They didn't agree with that though. If Ray was to drink with anyone it would be them, and they hadn't seen him.

Finally, knowing he was her last resort, she called Jack. It seemed to take a long time for him to answer his phone and she worried that maybe he'd stayed at the O'Neal's because of the storm but finally his sleepy voice came on the line.

"Hello?"

"Jack."

"Maggie?"

"Yes it's me," she choked back a sob.

"What time is it?"

"It's late, I mean early. Just after one."

His voice became more alert as he heard the urgency in her voice. "What is it, what's wrong?"

"Have you seen dad?"

"Ray? No, not since the night of the carols."

And with that Maggie started to cry and babble. "I thought he was coming to see you, because he was upset with you because of me, you see, because I was upset and he wanted to tell you off, even though I told him not to, but when I woke up he was gone so I figured that's where he went. But if he's not there and he's not here and his friends haven't seen him then where is he? There's a storm and it's raining and he's old and he hasn't come home."

"Maggie, slow down. Your father was coming to see me to tell me off?"

"That's what I thought, but if you haven't seen him where is he? Jack I'm so worried."

"Maggie, take a deep breath, I'm sure he's fine."

"He took the bike Jack, he's on that stupid old farm bike out in this storm."

"Ok," he said. "Right." Maggie could hear in his voice that he was thinking, and his voice had become authoritative. She relaxed into it, happy to let him take control because she herself had no clue what to do next.

"Stay put," Jack said. "I'll come to you and check the roads, see if there's any sign of him along there."

"I already drove along the roads, four times." Then she exclaimed loudly, "Oh! Why didn't I think of that before?"

"Think of what?"

"Sometimes he takes shortcuts across the farms to avoid Geoffrey. He might have done that tonight." Her voice choked up again. "Oh Jack, what if something bad has happened to him? What if he's lying out there in the rain and the dark all by himself, hurt?"

"Maggie." He spoke sternly to snap her out of the deep hole she had been about to descend into. "We'll find him. I promise."

She nodded, forgetting he couldn't see her.

"My car won't go on the farm," she said. "It'll get bogged down."

"My truck can do it. Just stay put and I'll be there shortly."

She nodded again.

Jack was as good as his word and not long after she saw headlights turn into the end of the driveway. Before he had even pulled completely up in front of the house she was out there, yanking on the door handle and climbing into the passenger seat.

"Nice jacket," he said, trying to lighten the mood. But Maggie didn't laugh, she couldn't even summon a smile. She just looked at him, all wide eyed and frightened and he felt the urge to reach over and pull her into his arms and kiss all her worries away. He knew though that the only thing that could make her feel better right then was having her father home, safe and sound. So he kept his hands on the steering wheel and quizzed her, "Which way?"

She pointed down the driveway, "down there and turn right. There's a farm about a half a kilometre along, he cuts through there."

Jack drove where she directed. When they reached a gate she told him to stop, then she jumped out of the truck and held the gate open for him to pass through. Then she closed it behind him and climbed back into the truck, pointing him forwards. So started a pattern, Jack driving through the paddocks, headlights on full beam and both of them calling out the windows into the rain, and when they reached the next gate Maggie would jump out and open it. They had driven through six paddocks and Jack was just starting to wonder how big this farm actually was and whether they were going to find themselves on the other side of the country when Maggie grabbed his arm.

"Stop! What's that?" she said, trying to peer through the rain.

Jack stepped on the brakes and tried to follow the direction of her finger. "Where?" he asked, but then he realised she was already out of the truck and running towards something lying in the grass twenty metres away. He stared at it for a moment and realised it was the wheels of a bike, lying on its side. Maggie was sprinting towards it.

Cursing, he reached for the door handle. He wished that he'd been able to get there first, just in case of the worst case scenario. He wanted to protect her from what she might find, and he was scared that if Ray had met his fate no amount of comforting from Jack or anyone else would help Maggie forget what she was about to see.

She was on the ground next to her father when he reached them and for the longest five seconds of his life he thought his fears had been confirmed. Ray was pale and still, eyes closed and body limp. He was wet through and covered in mud, and his legs were trapped beneath the bike. Maggie had dropped to her knees in the mud beside him and was staring at her father in horror.

"Dad?" she whimpered, but the wind snatched the word and carried it away.

"Move over Maggie," Jack shouted, "I have to get this bike off him." It took all Jack's strength to lift the bike and drop it to one side. While he did Maggie moved around to her father's head and lifted his shoulders into her lap. She leant over him to try and keep the rain off his face and stroked his hair.

"Dad," she said it louder and shook his shoulders.

Ray groaned and moved a hand weakly.

"He's alive!" Maggie cried out with relief, "Jack, he's breathing." She leant down to her father's face, "Dad! Dad can you hear me?"

"Of course I can hear you, you're screaming right in my ear," Ray grumbled.

"Oh dad, whatever possessed you to take the bike out? You could see a storm was coming."

"I was going to give that young man of yours a speaking too."

Maggie was acutely aware of Jack beside her. "He's not my young man, dad. And I told you to leave it alone."

"I just hate seeing you upset my girl."

Maggie kissed her father's forehead. "I know, and I love you for it. But you could have been killed. What would I have told Willow? And can you imagine what mum would say?"

Rays opened his eyes then. "Eh, we don't need to mention this to her do we?" There was genuine fear in his eyes. "She'll kill me for sure."

"Well you're still alive for now sir," Jack cut in, "and I think we should save this conversation for somewhere a little warmer and drier. We need to get you checked over at the hospital."

"*You*," Ray's eyes focused on Jack over Maggie's shoulder. "You've got some nerve showing your face here. This is all your fault you know."

"Dad, you can't blame Jack for your own stupidity. Besides, if it wasn't for him I would never have found you so you should be thanking him."

"Thank you," Ray mumbled grudgingly.

"You're very welcome," Jack said with a smile. Water was running down his face and his hair was plastered against his head. "Now let's get you to a hospital."

"I don't want to go to a hospital," Ray protested as Jack lifted the old man into his arms. Maggie couldn't help but admire how strong he was, and then rolled her eyes and

284

mentally scolded herself for thinking such thoughts at such an inappropriate time.

"Hey, you're a doctor," Ray pointed out as Jack carried him to the car. "Can't *you* just check me over? I'm telling you guys I feel fine."

"I'm a veterinarian. I deal with slightly different patients."

"We all share the same basic parts."

"All the same," Jack said as Maggie opened the back door of the truck and he laid Ray out on the back seat, "I'd prefer you checked out by a doctor." Jack reached over into the back and pulled out the blanket he kept there for when Rufus rode with him. "Sorry about the smell," he apologised to Ray as he tucked it around him, "but it will keep you warm at least."

He climbed into the driver's seat and turned the key in the ignition while Ray grumbled in the back. Jack had just backed the truck around to head back the way they had come when Ray shot bolt upright.

"Wait," he said, "what about my bike? We can't just leave it there."

Jack looked sideways at Maggie and lifted one eyebrow in question as if to say, 'are you going to deal with this?'

"That damn bike can stay there until it rusts into a scrap heap for all I care," Maggie said hotly to her father. "And I'm pretty sure mum will feel the same way."

Ray subsided on to the seat again. "You're not going to tell her about this are you love?"

"I don't really have a lot of choice do I? It's serious this time dad." She shivered; the adrenaline and the cold from the rain had caught up with her and she felt chilled to the bone.

"Traitor," Ray grumbled.

"Here," Jack shrugged off his jacket and passed it over to Maggie, "Drape this over your knees, it will help warm you back up." He fiddled with buttons on the dashboard and soon hot air was blowing from the vents and filling the inside of the truck, making it cosy. When they got back onto the main road Ray closed his eyes and drifted off to sleep, lulled like a baby by the rhythm of the trucks wheels. Maggie, who had been half turned in her seat to keep an eye on her father turned to face the front again, adjusting her seatbelt.

"Thank you," she said quietly to Jack.

"No problem," he took his eyes off the road for a brief moment to flash a smile. "It all worked out well in the end."

"Thanks to you. I wouldn't have been able to find him without your help. God knows how long he would have been lying out there," she shuddered.

"He's fine," Jack said soothingly, "he's a tough old guy."

"He is," Maggie nodded, "but at the same time he's also my frail old dad. I don't know what I'd do if I lost him."

"Don't think like that. He's strong, I'm sure he'll be with us for awhile yet."

"I hope so."

"I'm guessing he's where you get your strength from," Jack commented.

She turned to him in surprise. "Me? Strong? I don't think so. I nearly fell apart tonight, remember? I just don't cope well in situations like this."

"Hey, not many people could cope with a situation like tonight."

"You did."

'That's different. As fond as I am of the old guy, he's not my father." He flicked a glance in the rear view mirror at Ray and was satisfied to see him roll over a bit in his sleep. "Who knows how I would have handled it if it *had* been my father. I probably would have been just as upset as you were."

"Your dad is still alive?"

"Yes."

"And your mother?"

"Yes she's very much alive and well, not together with my father though. No she's currently on," he paused to work something out in his head, "husband number five, if I'm correct."

Maggie whistled. "Phew, that's quite a lot of husbands."

"Tell me about it. It's also more than enough step fathers. I have a feeling he won't be the last though."

Maggie was quiet for a minute and then she apologised softly. "I'm sorry I never took the time to find out more about your life. I've been pretty self centred haven't I?"

"It's fine, you had a lot on your plate. Besides," he smiled sideways at her again, "there's plenty of time for all that."

"There you go again."

"What?"

"Confusing me. For someone who keeps banging on about keeping things uncomplicated you sure do know how to mess with a girls head."

Jack looked at her in astonishment. "What on earth are you on about now?"

"Eyes on the road please, my father has already survived one vehicular accident today, let's not put him through a second."

He looked back at the road. "Only if you explain what you meant by that last statement, and quickly."

"Today at your office, you said we should leave each other alone so as not to complicate things. But just now you act as if you're still interested."

"That's because I *am* still interested."

"Then what was all that stuff you said today?"

"I *knew* you weren't listening. What I said was that we should just take a step backwards and slow things down a little, so as not to confuse things for your family and friends."

"*They* are not confused. The only person confused is *me*."

"When I said no to spending Christmas day with you Maggie it wasn't because I didn't want to, I can think of nowhere else I'd rather spend it."

"Then why?"

"I was thinking of you. At your ex-husbands wake I heard your mother telling you that people were gossiping – the curse of small towns like I told you when we first met by the way – about us. I didn't want anyone thinking bad things about you so I thought we should just cool it for awhile until the dust settles."

"You were just trying to protect me from this town's idle minds?"

He nodded.

"And that's the *only* reason you said all that stuff about us not seeing each other?"

He looked over at her again, his face serious. "Maggie I don't know how many times I can tell you this or how much clearer I can make it. *I like you*. I mean, I really, *really* like you. You fascinate the hell out of me and have done since the day you pointed a shotgun at my head."

Maggie flushed, she had forgotten all about that.

"I want to know everything there is to know about you," he continued. "Give me half a chance and I'll show you just how much I want to be with you."

"I thought you'd gone off me."

"Oh I tried," he joked and she slapped his arm. "But the thing with you Maggie, is that you're like a parasite. You've wormed your way right under my skin, and I have the suspicion that nothing I do is going to get you back out of there again."

"Wow, that's one of the most romantic things anyone has ever said to me."

"Seriously?"

"Of course not. It's disgusting."

He laughed.

"But I get where you're coming from," she admitted, "because for some reason I can't get you out of my head, even though you irritate the hell out of me."

"My pleasure."

"You know, I had you two pegged as fairly intelligent. But the way you've been acting lately I'm beginning to rethink."

Maggie swivelled around in her seat to look down at her father. "I thought you were asleep."

"Oh I'd much rather be, believe me, but you two kept yakking."

"Sorry."

"Don't be sorry, just sort your crap out. I can't keep up with you."

"Dad!"

"Well honestly, you're like one of those soap operas on the telly. One minute you like each other, the next minute you're spitting tacks. Well you are anyway," he pointed at Maggie. Then he turned the finger on Jack. "*You* seem a little more balanced."

Maggie turned back to Jack, embarrassed. "Sorry about him."

"He's kind of right though isn't he. I mean, we have been fairly annoying."

"Don't tell him that, he'll never shut up."

"I hate to break this moving talk up, lovebirds," Ray piped up from the backseat, "but you've just driven right past the hospital."

As it turned out, Ray was incredibly lucky not to do himself any great injury in his accident, coming out of it with only a mildly sprained ankle.

"You've been incredibly lucky," the doctor told him sternly. "If the ground hadn't been so muddy from the rain which helped cushion your fall, I could be zipping you into a body bag right now."

Ray hung his head in repentance.

"And fancy putting your daughter through the fright of her life like that," the doctor continued with the lecture "I've a good mind to give Dot a call when she gets home and let her know just what you've been up to."

Ray had looked up again quickly. "Aw no, please doc, there's no call for that. I've learnt my lesson. I won't ride the bike into town anymore." He gave the boy scouts salute with a flourish, regardless of the fact he'd never been to a meeting in his life.

"You won't get the chance," Maggie said, standing at the side of the bed while the doctor finished his examination. "First thing in the new year I'll be selling whatever's left of that damn thing."

Ray opened his mouth to protest but Maggie gave him a fierce look. "It's either that or I let the doc here call mum and she'll probably shove it off a cliff with you tied to it. At least my way you might get some money out of it."

Ray shut his mouth again and sighed deeply. He knew when he was beat.

The storm had blown out as quickly as it had blown in, and the sun was just blazing up over the horizon as Jack dropped them back at the house. He and Maggie hadn't had a chance to continue their conversation but he could see that it would have to wait. She was exhausted by the night's events.

He helped her assist Ray up the steps and onto the couch then he hovered, unsure.

"Dad, aren't you going to say thanks?" Maggie prompted.

"Thanks," Ray said. He was still smarting over the plans for his bike.

Maggie rolled her eyes. "He's grateful really." She walked Jack to the door. "We both are. And mum would be too, if she knew."

"You're not going to tell her, are you love? You promised." Ray's head popped up over the back of the couch.

Maggie frowned at him. "I promised no such thing. And funny how you heard that from all the way over there but you can't hear when I ask you to help with the dishes." Ray sank back down onto the couch, out of sight.

Jack grinned at Maggie. "I bet you can't stay mad at him for long."

Maggie sighed. "No you're probably right, but he doesn't have to know that."

"Are you going to tell your mother what happened?"

"Are you kidding? No way."

He looked over her shoulder, "Where is your mother by the way? And Willow?"

"It's a long story, but the short version is they're in a cave in the hills."

"Fine, don't tell me then."

"No seriously, they're in a cave somewhere up in the hills around the lake. With three of my mother's friends who also happen to be aged in their seventies but who, just like her, refuse to grow up."

"See," Jack said, "just when I think your family couldn't possibly get any more interesting, you go and tell me something like that. You must tell me more about this cave."

Maggie put her hand to her mouth to cover a yawn. "Another time. I just want to get my head down on my pillow and sleep for a few hours."

"Of course, I shouldn't be keeping you up." Jack leant forward and kissed her on the forehead lightly, "Is that invitation for Christmas day still open?"

"Hmm," Maggie pretended to consider it, then she smiled. "Of course it is."

"I'll see you tomorrow then. Sleep tight beautiful Maggie Tanner."

Then he left. Maggie watched him drive off down the driveway. His hand extended out of the window and waved as he turned out the end, and she waved back then shut the door. She yawned again and wandered over to check on her father. He was sound asleep, snoring lightly. Watching him for a few minutes she reflected on Jack's words; yes, her family might be as crazy as a box of feral cats, but they were her family. And despite their varying eccentricities she wouldn't trade them for anything.

Chapter twenty four

"Mum! Mum!" Maggie's eyes flew open when she heard Willow calling. She rolled over and looked at the clock, eleven. Only a few short hours since she had closed her eyes, but the sleep had done its job and she felt marginally more human.

"I'm in here baby," she called, stretching.

The door flew open with a crash and Maggie winced.

"What are you still doing in bed lazy bones?" Willow asked, puzzled.

"Never mind that, come over here and tell me all about your night. Did you have fun?"

Willow skipped across the room and jumped up onto the bed beside her mother.

"Ouuf," Maggie said, as she got an inadvertent knee in the stomach.

"Sorry."

Willow snuggled in beside her mother, on top of the covers. "I missed you," she admitted.

"I missed you too baby girl," Maggie pulled her in and kissed her daughters face in a series of fluttery kisses until Willow pushed her away, laughing.

"Stop, it tickles," she protested.

"So how was your night?"

"It was really cool mum. I know why Gran likes going there now; it was so much fun, like camping, but cooler."

"Did you get wet in the storm?"

"Nope, we were nice and dry inside the cave. Lois lit a fire so we were really warm."

"And what did you get up to?"

"Mum, you know as well as I do that what happens in the cave, stays in the cave. Gran told me you went when you were little and that you had to take the secret oath as well."

"Oh right," Maggie bit her lip to stop from grinning, "the secret oath. Yes I remember that. Ok I'll let you off from telling me anything. As long as you're ok and you had fun I'm happy with that."

"I did, and I'm fine. Although – " she pulled a face.

"What?"

"Well listening to Hazel sing was a bit like torture. She's terrible, almost as bad as you."

"Hey! You take that back." Maggie tickled Willow hard on her ribs until giggling, she apologised.

"Is it safe to come in?" a voice asked from out of sight around the door.

"Yes mum," Maggie said, "you can come in."

Dot entered the room, looking rueful. "You're not angry with me?"

"No I'm not angry, I'm *furious*. And if you *ever* take my daughter away again without first consulting me I will move out of this house and you will never see her again, are we clear?" But there was no real venom behind Maggie's words, they were more token as she reasserted her motherly authority.

"Crystal," Dot nodded with relief. "Why are you still in bed? And why is your father asleep on the couch?"

"It's a long story."

"Do I want to hear it?"

"No, it's probably best you don't."

Dot nodded. "I'll take your word for it."

"Right, time for you to get up, sleepyhead." Willow crawled off the bed and peeled the covers off Maggie. "Tomorrow is Christmas," Willow continued, "and you have so much to do."

"Like what?"

"Duh, like wrap lots of presents. There's only a couple under the tree and that can't be right."

"Cheeky," Dot swotted her. "Go and wake your grandfather up." She watched fondly as Willow ran from the room.

"I'm sorry I didn't ask you," she apologised again to Maggie. "I was afraid you would say no and after everything she's been through lately with the discovery of Jon and the funeral, I just figured she could do with a special little getaway."

"It's fine mum. I was pissed off at first but I know your intentions were good. Just promise to never take her away again without talking to me." Maggie's face became very serious. "That girl is everything to me. I don't know what I'd do if anything ever happened to her."

"Nothing is going to happen Maggie, she's fine and she's got all of us looking out for her. You're a wonderful mother, you really are."

"Thanks, it's nice to have it validated once in a while."

Mother and daughter shared a tender smile, then Dot checked her watch. "Willow is right, it's time to get out of bed. We have things to prepare for tomorrow." She was almost out the door when Maggie called after her.

"Mum?"

"Yes?"

"We have an extra guest for Christmas, I hope that's ok."

"Of course it is, the more the merrier. Anyone I know?"

Maggie looked down at the bedspread and fiddled with a loose string. "Jack," she said quietly.

"Sorry, I couldn't quite catch that, who?"

"I said Jack and you heard me perfectly. You're just making me repeat it to be mean."

A glint appeared in Dot's eye. "Oh wonderful," she said. "I take it things are back on track?"

"We're friends again, yes, if that's what you mean."

"Friends?"

"Yes, friends."

"That's it?"

"That's it."

"Nothing more on the cards?"

"Well now, I didn't say *that* exactly."

"I'll just watch this space then shall I?"

"You do that."

The rest of the day passed in a flurry of present wrapping, food preparation and house tidying. The scents of cinnamon and nutmeg mingled with the scent of pine from the tree. Last night's storm was a distant memory and the land, washed clean, basked in the heat from a hot, summer sun. Willow vanished as soon as she knew there were chores to be done, and did not return until the sun was going down on Christmas Eve. The four of them ate salad and cold chicken on the porch, and then went inside to enjoy a drink and watch The Grinch who stole Christmas. It was cosy and soul warming and Maggie felt like she might burst open from the happiness that swelled up inside.

Chapter twenty five

Christmas morning, as if in an effort to make up for its failure the day of the storm, the sun turned the heat on early and by eight the road was blurry with a heat haze hovering just above the surface and the smell of hot tarmac had started to pervade the air. Maggie knew this because she had looked down the driveway towards the road at least twelve times since rising. Each time on the pretence of doing something else, like throwing a tea towel in the laundry hamper, or fetching the mail, despite the fact the mailman almost never delivered before one in the afternoon and certainly never at all on holidays.

"What?" she asked defensively when her mother and father exchanged glances upon her return to the house.

"Nothing," they both chorused.

The four of them exchanged presents and drank a glass of bubbly wine with breakfast, which consisted of bacon and eggs, hash browns and French toast.

"Oh hell," Ray groaned afterwards, holding the sides of his stomach, "and it's only just begun."

Finally, at just after eleven, the sound of tyres crunching over gravel could be heard and Maggie came flying out from her room where she had been checking her outfit, also for the twelfth time that morning. She came to a halt when she saw her family watching her.

"I think Jack might be here," she said, trying to sound casual.

"Well you'd best go check then, hadn't you?" said Ray.

"You know, just to be polite and hospitable," Dot added.

"After all," Ray said, "he may have forgotten where the door is."

They grinned at each other again like they were the funniest people on the planet.

"I'm going to bang your heads together if you two keep grinning at each other like that," Maggie warned.

"Like what?" Dot protested innocently. "Can we help it if we're happy? It's Christmas after all."

"You know exactly what. And you'd better not say anything stupid in front of Jack. Not unless you want secrets to start popping up out of the woodwork." She looked meaningfully at Ray when she said it. His face blanched.

"I'll behave," he said.

"Secrets? What secrets?" Dot asked. "What's she on about?"

But Maggie had already left the room, walking at a more normal pace out onto the porch to greet Jack. She waited at the top of the stairs while he parked under the shade of the

Magnolia tree. Willow and Nick were taking turns to push each other on the tyre swing, although from what Maggie had observed that morning it seemed to be Nick who was doing most of the pushing. Nick's family weren't overly into Christmas. They did the present thing and ate a big breakfast and then that was them done for the day. She saw Jack get out of the truck and exchange words with Willow and Nick, though she couldn't hear what from where she was standing. She saw Willow roll her eyes and shake her head as if Jack had said something lame. Jack opened the door wider and Rufus bounded out and over to Willow, jumping up to place his paws on her shoulders and lick her face. Maggie could hear Willow giggling from where she stood and the sound warmed her heart. Jack looked up and saw Maggie watching and waved. She waved back and tried to ignore the fact that her heart had started beating a whole lot faster.

God he was good looking. She didn't know how she had ever thought otherwise. She pretended she was picking splinters out of the wood on the railing while he walked over.

"Merry Christmas," he smiled, coming up to stand beside her.

"Merry Christmas to you too," she said back, although she didn't turn to look at him, watching Willow and Nick instead. She felt both nervous and excited to see him again.

"Get anything good?" he asked.

She struggled to remember, the now familiar smell of him standing so close had made her feel light headed.

"A book from mum and dad and a pretty photo frame from Willow. You?"

"Oh Rufus presented me with an old sock in bed this morning."

"Oh that's, um, *lovely*. Very thoughtful of him."

"Not really, he gives me the same thing every year. Doesn't go to a lot of trouble, just steals one from the laundry basket."

"Cute."

"Here," he handed her a small parcel.

"What is it?"

"Traditionally, I think you're meant to unwrap it to find out rather than ask the giver."

She ran a fingernail under the tape and peeled back the paper to reveal an unmistakable small jewellery box.

"Oh," she said. "I couldn't possibly accept this."

"How do you know when you haven't even opened it? It might be a walnut for all you know."

"A walnut?"

"First thing I could think of."

"So it's not a walnut? Now I'll be disappointed."

"Hopefully when you do eventually open it, you won't be."

She lifted the lid and frowned. It was a sterling silver necklace with a pendant in the shape of a witch on a broom. "A witch?" She didn't grasp the significance.

"Don't you like it? I thought with you being so magical yourself you would."

"You think I'm a witch?"

He smiled. "How else could you have cast such a spell over me?"

She smiled, touched. It was the most romantic thing anyone had ever bought her. She wasn't about to tell him that though. "You get away with corny lines like that back where you come from?"

"Oh yes. City girls lap up stuff like that."

"Just how many girls are we talking about here, for interests' sake?"

"Not too many. The usual amount. May I?" He gestured towards the case and she handed it over. He took the necklace out, placing the case down on the banister beside him.

Maggie turned her back to him and lifted her hair with one hand while he threaded the necklace around her neck and fastened the clasp. His fingers lightly tickled the fine hairs on the back of her neck and she felt them stand up involuntarily. She closed her eyes and enjoyed the sensation of being so close to him again.

Jack was also enjoying the lack of space between them, and without a thought he leant forward and touched his lips to the back of her neck. He felt her shiver.

"Mmm," he murmured. "You smell delicious, what *is* that intoxicating smell?"

"Lilac soap," she told him, turning back to face him. She wondered if he would remember handing her the soap that day in her shop and the meaning on the card.

His eyebrows shot up, which indicated to her that he did. She blushed slightly.

"Wait here," she told him, and hurried inside to fetch her own present for him. When she returned she seemed almost reluctant to pass him the parcel.

"I'm sorry but it's nothing as fancy as a necklace," she apologised. She'd bought it as a tongue in cheek gift but now she was regretting her choice.

"I'm sure whatever it is I'll love it." He opened the paper and then it was his turn to frown at her quizzically.

She reached over and pulled out the heavy duty green rubber gardening gloves.

"They're for next time Bruno comes in to see you, so you don't get scratched again."

He laughed. "What a thoughtful gift. Thank you."

"You're very welcome. I know you don't share my special animal whispering talent, so I thought these might help you deal with him."

"I'm sure they'll come in very handy."

"Merry Christmas Jack."

"And Merry Christmas to you too, beautiful Maggie Tanner." He replied softly, reaching out a hand to brush some hair from her face. "May I?"

She nodded.

He leant forward and kissed her, softly at first then hungrily. The only thing that stopped Maggie pushing him back against the wall of the house and ravishing him right there was the sound of groans and fake vomiting from Willow and Nick. She pushed Jack away and put a hand to her mouth.

"Oh god I forgot they were there," she said, horrified. This wasn't how she planned on Willow finding out, but when she looked at her daughter there was no shock on her face. Instead she smiled at her mother and gave her the thumbs up to signify her approval.

"Get a room!" Nick called and Willow punched him hard on the upper arm.

Dot's head appeared in the doorframe. "Grubs up!" she called. "Oh hi Jack, I didn't know you'd arrived," she said, her face a picture of innocence. "Merry Christmas to you."

"Merry Christmas to you too Dot."

"You hungry? There's a feast laid out inside. Ray is chomping to get started, despite already inhaling his body weight in bacon at breakfast. I swear, that man does this every year. He'll eat himself fit to burst then complain all the night long how sick he is. Then he'll get up tomorrow and start eating all the leftovers. He hates to waste any food you see."

"Let me see if I can help him out with that. I'm pretty hungry myself and the smells you've bought out with you are causing my taste buds to leap right off my tongue."

"Good boy," Dot nodded. "I do like a man with an appetite. So does Maggie by the way, she's an excellent cook."

"Mum!"

"What? Did I say something wrong?"

Jack hid a smile. "Lead the way."

"Oi! You two! Get in here now or I'll lock this door and you'll miss out altogether," Dot called to Willow and Nick.

"Yeah right!" Willow hollered back.

The adults were seated around the table when Willow and Nick finally came running inside, tripping and elbowing each other to be the first to get to the table. They fought over the same chair but a swift kick from Willow won out and Nick collapsed into the other one, hurt and nursing his pride.

'Lift it, don't scrape it."

"No you don't, you two," Dot scowled.

"What?"

"Didn't we raise you better than that? Scram and wash your hands, the pair of you."

Nick and Willow took off out of the room, jostling to see who could get to the stairs first.

Dot watched them go and nodded to herself happily.

"Oh yes," she said to no one in particular, "it's fairly obvious what's going to happen with those two." Then she caught sight of Maggie's expression and hastily added, "Oh far, *far* in the future. Obviously."

Printed in Great Britain
by Amazon

30517458R00178